A Bridal Bouquet Bump-Off

Heavenly Highland Inn Cozy Mystery Series

Cindy Bell

Copyright © 2015 Cindy Bell
All rights reserved.

All rights reserved. No part of this publication may be reproduced or transmitted in any form or by any means, electronic or mechanical, including photocopy, recording, or any information storage or retrieval system, without permission in writing from the publisher.

This is a work of fiction. The characters, incidents and locations portrayed in this book and the names herein are fictitious. Any similarity to or identification with the locations, names, characters or history of any person, product or entity is entirely coincidental and unintentional.

All trademarks and brands referred to in this book are for illustrative purposes only, are the property of their respective owners and not affiliated with this publication in any way. Any trademarks are being used without permission, and the publication of the trademark is not authorized by, associated with or sponsored by the trademark owner.

ISBN-13: 978-1507851371

ISBN-10: 1507851375

More Cozy Mysteries by Cindy Bell

Dune House Cozy Mystery Series

Seaside Secrets

Boats and Bad Guys

Treasured History

Hidden Hideaways

Dodgy Dealings

Heavenly Highland Inn Cozy Mystery Series

Murdering the Roses

Dead in the Daisies

Killing the Carnations

Drowning the Daffodils

Suffocating the Sunflowers

Books, Bullets and Blooms

A Deadly serious Gardening Contest

Wendy the Wedding Planner Cozy Mystery Series

Matrimony, Money and Murder

Chefs, Ceremonies and Crimes

Knives and Nuptials

Bekki the Beautician Cozy Mystery Series

Hairspray and Homicide

A Dyed Blonde and a Dead Body

Mascara and Murder

Pageant and Poison

Conditioner and a Corpse

Mistletoe, Makeup and Murder

Hairpin, Hair Dryer and Homicide

Blush, a Bride and a Body

Shampoo and a Stiff

Cosmetics, a Cruise and a Killer

Lipstick, a Long Iron and Lifeless

Camping, Concealer and Criminals

Table of Contents

Chapter One 1

Chapter Two 19

Chapter Three 38

Chapter Four 55

Chapter Five 72

Chapter Six 82

Chapter Seven 99

Chapter Eight 112

Chapter Nine 127

Chapter Ten 149

Chapter Eleven 174

Chapter One

The Heavenly Highland Inn was quiet for the moment. Vicky knew that it wouldn't last long. There were always new guests arriving, and with Aunt Ida never far away something zany was always happening. But for the moment Vicky was alone with her thoughts, which just happened to be filled with her upcoming nuptials. As Vicky thumbed through the photographs in her hand she couldn't help but smile. They were pictures of the party tent she had ordered to put up in the garden of the Heavenly Highland Inn. Her heart was so full of anticipation that she thought it might burst. Although she had been planning parties for quite some time as the event director at the Heavenly Highland Inn, this particular celebration meant the most to her. It was her very own wedding.

Vicky closed her eyes and smiled widely as she thought of Mitchell, her soon to be husband. She could remember the first day she met him, with his fierce blue eyes and his deep southern accent. She remembered being a little unsettled by the intensity of the way he looked at her, and at the same time thrilled. As their relationship developed, she felt as if she was the luckiest woman in the world to have found him.

Mitchell had worked hard as a deputy sheriff to earn his new title of detective, and throughout all of their ups and downs Mitchell had never once given her a reason not to trust him. She kept putting things off, kept resisting the truth that she had fallen hopelessly in love, but he never backed down. He had been determined that she would love him, what he didn't know was that he didn't have to work so hard, she knew now, looking back, that she had fallen in love with him the very first time she had looked into his eyes.

Now, she was going to marry him in the very inn that her parents had run for so many years before their tragic deaths in a car accident. Vicky was certain that she would feel their presence all around her as she took her walk down the aisle. It gave her a slight twinge of pain to think of walking down the aisle without her father by her side. It was a truth she had faced a long time ago. Her sister, Sarah, had been able to walk down the aisle with their father, but Vicky wouldn't have that opportunity. It made her ache a little for the past, but she was so excited about the future, that she pushed it from her mind. She was just about to go through the instructions for setting up the party tent once more, when her thoughts were interrupted by the boisterous voice of her aunt.

"What are you talking about? I said nothing about bluebirds, I want doves, at least a dozen!" Ida's shrill voice carried through the lobby of the Heavenly Highland Inn. Vicky looked up nervously as her aunt walked towards her. Ida was dressed in an outlandish outfit that incorporated an orange leather skirt and what looked like a pineapple pattern on her blouse. Vicky had to lower her eyes to keep from giggling. "Get it right," Ida demanded before she hung up the phone. Ida was in her sixties, though she could easily be mistaken for being in her forties. She was a spry and daring woman who had never let anything in life slow her down. She had always been Vicky's role model.

"Doves, Aunt Ida?" Vicky asked as she looked up at her with a grin.

"Doves, of course doves," Ida shrugged. "We can't have you getting married without doves."

"Oh no," Vicky groaned and shook her head. "I don't want doves, Aunt Ida. Think of the mess!"

"Vicky," Ida sighed and looked her niece in the eyes. "You are going to have the most amazing wedding. I promise. But there will be doves."

"Fine, but only two," Vicky relented. "We can't have a dozen doves getting loose and landing on the wedding cake, now can we?" she asked pleadingly.

"Speaking of the wedding cake," Ida pressed forward without actually answering her question. "Is it ready yet?"

"Chef Henry is working on it," Vicky assured her.

"I hope he remembered to add the musical element before he began layering it," Ida said with a cluck of her tongue.

"Musical element, what musical element?" Vicky asked as she narrowed her eyes.

"Well, you said no to the fountain in the middle, so I decided it would be nice if we had a musical cake," Ida explained. "I saw one on this show I was watching the other day. The moment the cake is cut into, a lovely melody begins to play. How delightful, hmm?"

"Oh Aunt Ida, I don't know," Vicky sighed. She made a mental note to discuss the cake with Chef Henry and make sure that there was no musical element involved. "I really want to keep this fairly simple," Vicky explained.

"Sorry sweetie, but there isn't going to be anything simple about this wedding," Ida insisted. "You only get married once, and I'm here to make sure it goes off with a bang!"

"Aunt Ida," Vicky tried again in a rational tone. "What exactly do you mean by bang?" she asked as she narrowed her eyes.

"Relax Vicky, Ida is doing a wonderful job," Mitchell said as he stepped up beside Ida. Vicky hadn't even noticed him come through the entrance of the lobby. As a detective he could be like that, quiet as a ninja.

"Mitchell," Vicky smiled. "I was just trying to tell Aunt Ida that we are interested in keeping things simple."

"Simple?" he said as he wrapped an arm around Ida's shoulders. He pretended to look very confused. "But there will be doves, right?" he asked.

"Yes," Ida said quickly and giggled. "At least twenty."

"Twenty?" Mitchell grimaced and looked from Vicky back to Ida again. "Are you sure that will be enough?"

"Oh, you two," Vicky said with a roll of her eyes and a shake of her head.

"Well, I'm off to finalize some plans," Ida said as she waved to the couple.

"Aunt Ida, I mean it, no fireworks!" Vicky called after her. Ida hurried off. Vicky knew she was likely to claim that she hadn't heard a word that Vicky said. She sighed and turned back to Mitchell.

"Mitchell, did you get the flight numbers for your family?" she asked, hoping to change the subject.

"Yes, I did," Mitchell replied. "They will be here by eight o'clock tonight."

"So, we could have a late dinner?" Vicky suggested anxiously. She had never met Mitchell's family before. She knew that his mother and father were very traditional, and his sister and brother were accustomed to a southern lifestyle. Vicky wasn't sure whether any of them would be accepting of her. Mitchell didn't have to worry, as he already knew Vicky's entire family, which was very small. Her older sister, Sarah, was the co-owner of the inn. Her husband and two sons were always around. Then there was Ida, who had practically taken over as a parent to Sarah and Vicky after their parents passed away. They all loved Mitchell. Vicky wondered if it would be the same way with Mitchell's family.

"Maybe," Mitchell said with a slight frown. "It might be too late, I'll let you know for sure one way or the other once they land," he offered.

"Okay," Vicky nodded. "I already asked Chef Henry to prepare something."

"Thank you," he smiled and leaned across the desk to kiss her gently. When he pulled away he was still grinning. "Don't worry, Vicky, they're going to love you," Mitchell assured her fondly.

"Easy for you to say," she pouted. "You already love me."

"You're easy to love," he smiled at her. "So, you're sure that you're okay with the bachelor party being so far away?"

"I think it's perfect," Vicky nodded. "It will give Aunt Ida, Sarah, and me time to set up for the wedding."

"Doesn't seem fair that I get to have fun, and you'll be working," Mitchell pointed out.

"Planning our wedding is fun to me," Vicky smiled at him. "I couldn't think of anything I'd rather do."

"I'm sure it will be amazing," Mitchell nodded.

A man walked into the lobby of the inn and Mitchell waved to him. "I wanted to introduce you to someone," Mitchell said as he stepped to the side. "This is the new deputy sheriff. I'm showing him the ropes. Arthur, this is my fiancée, Vicky."

"Nice to meet you," Arthur said stiffly. His eyes were flicking in all directions around the inn. Vicky watched him for a moment, and then began to get a little dizzy from how fast he shifted his gaze.

"Nice to meet you as well, Arthur," she said. "I'm glad you will be here to keep us all safe while Mitchell is away partying."

Mitchell smiled and adjusted his hat on top of his sandy brown hair. "Just a little send off," he said.

"Sure," Arthur nodded without looking at him. "But with the Sheriff, a detective, and two other officers from the town's police force going, it will be prime time for crime in Highland," he crossed his arms. "Don't worry, nothing is going to get past me," he said sternly.

Mitchell clapped Arthur lightly on the shoulder. "He's a bit, enthusiastic," he stated with a chuckle.

"Never a bad idea to stay aware of your surroundings," Arthur pointed out, still in a very serious tone. Vicky raised an eyebrow at Mitchell and then smiled at Arthur.

"So, what brings you to Highland, Arthur?" Vicky asked casually.

"My wife," Arthur said glumly. Vicky was a little startled by his response. "She inherited a house," he explained. "A big old place with plenty of land. So, here I am," he flashed a strained smile.

"Not a happy move, I take it," Vicky said slowly as she studied him.

"Not exactly but we have to stay for the moment," he replied. "No offense, but I'm used to a city with a larger population than Highland."

"I understand," Vicky nodded. "I'd imagine it would be difficult to adjust to the country lifestyle around here when you're used to a bigger place," she smiled. "But I'm sure that once you get used to it, you won't want to trade it." Vicky had grown up in Highland and she had always loved the place. When she was away at college or travelled she always appreciated Highland more when she returned. "Just give it a little time," she suggested.

"I think it would take more time than I have left on this earth," Arthur countered with a shake of his head. "I think that there are more cows than people in this place."

Vicky smiled. "Trust me, there's more action in this sleepy little town than you realize."

"I guess I'll have to take your word for it," Arthur sighed.

"You've already made an arrest," Mitchell reminded him.

"Just one, and I've already been here a couple of weeks," Arthur said with a sigh.

"Let's go get you more familiar with some of the hot spots around town, Arthur," Mitchell suggested. "Vicky, I'll call you as soon as my family lands, okay?"

"Please do," Vicky smiled at him. As she watched the two walk out of the inn she was still surprised by the knowledge that she would soon be Mrs. Slate. She hadn't expected to like the sound of it so much. With Ida's hand in every little detail about the wedding, Vicky decided that she better check in with Chef Henry before her wedding cake ended up like a three story erupting volcano, or worse.

***

When Vicky stepped into the kitchen she was greeted by the lovely scent of vanilla. Chef Henry was bent over a sketch book on the butcher's block in the center of the large kitchen. He was an amazing chef, and Vicky had never come across anything he made that didn't taste delicious. She felt lucky that he was the one creating her wedding cake. Henry looked up at the sound of her footsteps on the tiled floor.

"Don't worry, Vicky," he said before she could even speak. "I'm not making a musical cake."

"Oh good," she laughed and leaned against the counter. "I know Aunt Ida can get a little over the top with these things."

"Only because she loves you," he pointed out with a warm smile. "Here, this is what I'm doing," he said as he pushed a sketch book towards Vicky.

"Henry," Vicky gasped as she looked at the tiered cake. It had three layers. On each layer a different flower from the garden was featured. On the very top of the cake there was a heart shaped cake topper. It was the perfect classic cake with amazing decorations. "It's beautiful," she sighed.

"This is a very special day for you, Vicky," Henry said with warmth in his eyes as he looked at her. "Nothing will ruin it."

"Nothing," Vicky agreed. She wanted to believe it. But there was a nagging in the back of her mind. She was so excited about the ceremony, and the life she would begin with Mitchell after, that it was hard not to be a little nervous that something could go wrong.

The biggest thing she had to be concerned about at the moment was how she would get along with Mitchell's family. She knew they had a very different lifestyle than she was accustomed to. They were more traditional in belief and in life choices. Mitchell's mother was a stay-at-home mom, his father worked as a carpenter. Vicky wasn't sure how they'd react to their son marrying a woman who didn't even think she wanted to get married not long before. She wasn't exactly traditional. Though she loved her nephews, she wasn't sure if she wanted children of her own. Though she loved Mitchell, she valued her time and the parts of her life that were separate from him. She was proud of her event planning, and of her role in running the inn. She wasn't sure if that was something that the rest of Mitchell's family would understand.

"Nothing," Henry repeated and reached out to ruffle Vicky's brown hair lightly. "So, get that worry out of your eyes before you make wrinkles."

"Oh no, wrinkles?" Vicky laughed. "Now, I really am worried."

Henry chuckled at her sarcasm. "Seriously though, Vicky, this is your time to enjoy yourself. Don't get caught up in the little things, just remember that when all of this is over, you get Mitchell for life!"

"Oh yes, that is a nice take-home gift," Vicky giggled. "Thanks Henry, I needed this chat."

"That's what I'm here for," he winked at her and turned back to his plans for the cake. "A few final details to smooth out, but I've already started it and it will be ready to go in plenty of time for the ceremony."

"Thanks again, Henry," Vicky said before she walked out of the kitchen. She took a deep breath and did her best to take Henry's advice. She didn't want to miss out on such a wonderful experience.

As she walked towards the lobby she ran into Sarah who had a concerned look on her face,

"There you are?" Sarah said.

"Is something wrong," Vicky asked with concern.

"Not really. I was just hoping you had some time to help me with the centerpieces," Sarah said with a sweet smile.

"I thought those were done!" Vicky said with surprise.

"I thought they were, too. But apparently three year olds like to unravel ribbons," she grimaced. "I think that we need to touch them up a bit."

"Oh, Rory just wanted to add his touch to the wedding," Vicky laughed. "We'll make sure we put them in a high place when we're done with them."

"Like that will stop him," Sarah said with a roll of her eyes. As the sisters walked to the lobby of the inn, Vicky felt her excitement growing. By the time they finished with the centerpieces it was time for Sarah to head home to her husband, Phil. He took care of the kids most weekends while she ran the inn, but it was his turn for a break as he was going on the bachelor trip tomorrow.

"I'll be back in a few hours," Sarah said. "With the kids of course. I'm going to feed them first and I'll have to make sure that Phil remembered to pack everything he needs for when they leave tomorrow."

"It's only an overnight trip," Vicky reminded

her.

"You'd be surprised how high maintenance that man is," Sarah laughed and waved to her sister as she walked towards the door. "Good luck with Mitchell's family," she said over her shoulder. "Not that you need it, they'll love you." Vicky sighed. She hoped that would prove to be true.

Chapter Two

Vicky tried to keep herself busy by double checking the seating chart so she wouldn't get nervous thinking about Mitchell's family. When she finished going through the chart she glanced at her watch. It was a little after eight and she still hadn't heard from Mitchell. She decided to check on the rooms that his family would be staying in one last time. Once she was sure they were perfect, she returned to the lobby. Her phone began to ring. Vicky picked it up as soon as she saw that it was Mitchell.

"Vicky," he said breathlessly into the phone. "I'm sorry I forgot to call, we'll be there in about ten minutes."

"Ten minutes?" Vicky gulped. "Okay, I'll check on dinner."

"Great," Mitchell said with relief. "They haven't eaten," he confirmed before hanging up.

Vicky didn't often hear Mitchell frazzled but

she could tell that he was a little overwhelmed. She ducked quickly into the kitchen.

"Henry, have you been able to throw something together for Mitchell's family?" she asked hopefully.

"Of course," Henry smiled as he lifted the lid off a pot roast. "All of the fixings," he promised.

"Henry, you're a lifesaver," she said with a sigh.

"Just remember that when I ask you for a raise," he cocked an eyebrow. Vicky smiled sweetly. "Taste?" he offered.

"I don't have time," Vicky said. "I have to touch up my make-up and make sure that the lobby is straightened up, and oh no, what if they are expecting to use the pool?"

"It's almost nine o'clock, I don't think they'll want to use the pool," Henry laughed. "Relax Vicky, remember, wrinkles!"

Vicky groaned and hurried into the lobby. She didn't have time to check her make-up, or straighten up the lobby, because she saw the flash of Mitchell's headlights as he pulled into the parking lot of the inn. Vicky could barely take a breath as her heart was racing so fast. She wasn't sure if she was going to be able to speak when she met them. She obviously knew about Mitchell's family as he often spoke about them, but she had also grilled him about them over the past few days so she could know as much about them as possible. Mitchell's parents were John and Mae-Ellen. His older sister was named Maisy, and his brother, Connor, was only a year younger than him.

The group bustled into the lobby of the inn with more noise than Vicky had ever heard anyone enter a room. When John dropped the bags on the floor, they thumped and clattered. When Mae-Ellen adjusted her purse it jangled and she grunted beneath the weight of it. When Maisy stumbled across the threshold of the door she fell into her brother, Connor, who nearly lost his footing and grabbed hold of the tourist lobby stand to catch his balance. As a result more than half of the brochures fell off the shelf and fluttered to the ground.

"Maisy, watch it!" Connor complained and dropped his suitcase on the floor as well.

"I've got it," Mitchell said as he caught a few of the brochures. Vicky walked around to the front of the desk and smiled as warmly as she could. The truth was, she was terrified. She had never met the family of any of her boyfriends before, her previous relationships had never been serious enough to reach that stage. Mitchell was much more than a boyfriend. She was going to spend the rest of her life with him.

"Hi, I'm Vicky..." she started to say.

"Oh, Vicky!" Mae-Ellen cried out and lunged towards her. Unfortunately, her foot got caught in the strap of one of the suitcases that had been tossed onto the floor. She nearly tackled Vicky. Luckily Vicky was strong enough to hold them both up. "Look at me, I'm such a fool, I'm so sorry," Mae-Ellen said as she straightened up. She smoothed down the skirt of her simple, blue flowered dress. Vicky found herself adoring the woman in that moment.

"Don't worry," Vicky assured her. "I'm just so happy to meet you."

"And we're happy to meet you, young lady," Mitchell's father said as he took his wife's arm and helped her get her footing. "Mitchell has told us so much about you."

"Oh, that's nice to hear," Vicky said warmly. "I've heard a lot about all of you as well."

"I bet," Connor said with a small smile.

"All good things," Vicky promised him.

"Now, that I don't believe," John chuckled.

"It's true, Dad," Mitchell said and smiled. "I didn't want to scare her off with the real stories."

The entire group laughed, including Vicky. She was feeling even more relaxed.

"Are you hungry?" Vicky asked as she looked

between John and Mae-Ellen.

"Oh honey, I'm hungry enough to even eat something that Mitchell's cooked!" Mae-Ellen announced.

"Ha ha," Mitchell said but he had a serious expression.

Mae-Ellen smiled as she looked at her son. "Well, I guess I'm not really that hungry," she laughed.

"Mom, don't tease, Mitchy," Maisy said as she stepped up beside her mother. "You know he takes everything too seriously."

"I do not," Mitchell responded defensively.

"Mitchy, calm down," Connor instructed him with a roll of his eyes.

"Watch it, Connor," Mitchell warned.

"Boys," John snapped. "Enough! There are ladies present."

Vicky stared at the gathering of Slates with a mixture of shock and affection. For some unknown reason she expected them to be prim and proper but instead they were a warm, relaxed family.

"Let's eat," she suggested, hoping to ease the tension that was building between the siblings.

"Yes, let's," Mae-Ellen agreed. "Hungry Slates are angry Slates."

As they walked towards the restaurant, Mitchell lingered back to walk beside Vicky. He looked into her eyes with a shy grin. "Sorry about that."

"Don't worry about it, Mitchy," Vicky said with a wicked smile.

"Don't even," Mitchell warned sharply.

"Mitchell, don't take things so seriously," Vicky said with a laugh and darted off ahead of him before he could get his arms around her. As they gathered in the restaurant, Vicky was pleased to see that Henry had pushed two tables together to accommodate the entire family. He really went out of his way to make sure that Vicky would have a good first dinner with her future in-laws.

"Oh, well that smells delicious!" Mae-Ellen said happily as she settled into one of the chairs. The scent of the pot roast was already drifting into the room. "Really, Vicky you didn't have to go to so much trouble."

"Actually the inn's chef, Henry, prepared dinner," Vicky said graciously as Henry brought out a tray and placed it on the table.

"A chef?" Mae-Ellen asked as she looked over Henry. "Don't you cook, Vicky?" she looked directly at Vicky. Vicky glanced guiltily over the beautiful meal that Henry had prepared. There was the pot roast with carrots and potatoes. He had also prepared fresh rolls, home-churned butter, and even a mixture of summer squash.

"I do," Vicky stumbled out. "I mean not very well," she added as she glanced over at Mitchell for help.

"Vicky cooks lovely meals," Mitchell said smoothly. "But with so much to plan for the wedding, I hardly think she'd have time to cook anything."

"Good point," Maisy nodded. "Speaking of the wedding, do you need any help with the decorations?" Maisy asked with a wide smile. "I'd love to help."

"Oh, thank you, that's wonderful, Maisy," Vicky said. "I'll let you know if we do. I think right now we have everything under control. My sister, Sarah, and I finished the centerpieces earlier today."

"That's right, your sister," Mae-Ellen grinned. "She's the one with two little boys, right?"

"Yes," Vicky smiled proudly. "She's bringing them over later."

"Look at that Mitchy, you've got a good chance of getting a little boy out of this one," Mae-Ellen said happily. Vicky felt her face drain of warmth. She tried to force a smile on her lips.

"Mom, you know we talked about this," Mitchell said impatiently.

27

"Oh, I know, I know. Trust me, many a young woman thinks she'd rather not have kids, but once that clock starts ticking," she clucked her tongue in the rhythm of a clock.

Vicky stared down at her food. She had to hold her tongue. She didn't want to upset Mae-Ellen.

"Mom," Mitchell said sternly. "You've got to back off about grandkids. It will happen if and when it happens."

"I know," Mae-Ellen sighed and waved her hand dramatically. "But these two are taking forever to find anyone," she glanced at Maisy and Connor who both looked away awkwardly. "So, for now, you're just going to have to be my only hope, Mitchell."

Vicky squirmed in her seat. She noticed that Connor was picking edgily at his pot roast. He muttered something to John, who nodded with a sly smirk.

"Is the food okay?" Vicky asked nervously.

"We're just used to eating things a little rarer," John explained.

"If it doesn't bleed, it's not what we need," Connor joked.

"Oh," Vicky's eyes widened. "Well, I can have Henry fix something else."

"Please no, that man has done enough," Mae-Ellen said. "It must be after hours for him."

"He doesn't mind," Vicky tried to assure them.

"Of course he wouldn't tell you if he did," Maisy pointed out. "You being the boss and all."

"Well, that's not exactly how we run things around here," Vicky explained quickly. "We're more of a family."

"Sure," Maisy nodded and took a bite of the potatoes. She smiled politely as she swallowed it, but Vicky noticed that she didn't take another bite.

"I can't wait to have some desert," John said

as he slapped his rounded belly lightly. "I know that will hit the spot."

Vicky froze. She hadn't thought to ask Henry to prepare a desert. Her heart began to race.

"Oh well, I'm sure we have some ice cream, or something," she said with defeat.

"Don't go to any trouble now," Mae-Ellen said and cast a look in Maisy's direction. Maisy pursed her lips and looked across the table at Connor. Connor pushed his plate back, still nearly full.

"I wasn't that hungry anyway," he said with a shrug.

Vicky stood up and rushed into the kitchen. With Henry's help she threw together some bowls of ice cream and gathered as many toppings as she could. As soon as she returned to the restaurant, the entire family cheered. They all seemed to be quite pleased with the selection. Vicky wanted to feel relieved, but she didn't. She was sure that she had made a very poor first impression. Once everyone had their fill of ice cream and Vicky had cleaned up, Mitchell met her in the kitchen.

"How are you doing?" he asked as he slid his arm around her waist and pulled her close to him.

"Not great," Vicky admitted and looked up into his eyes.

"Why not?" he asked with concern. "Aren't you excited about the wedding?"

"I am, but I don't think your family is," Vicky frowned.

"I think you're over thinking things," Mitchell said in a practical tone. "I warned you about my family, they're a little off center, but they grow on you."

"I'm not worried about liking them, I'm worried about them liking me," Vicky pointed out. "Do you think they like me?" Vicky asked with a grimace.

"Of course they do," Mitchell assured her. "I haven't seen my mother smile that wide in years."

"Sure, because she was laughing at me," Vicky

pointed out. "No one liked the food, and there wasn't any desert."

"Vicky, you need to stop worrying so much. I adore you, my family will adore you. So, just relax, sweetheart," he looked into her eyes intently. "We're all going to be family soon, Vicky. I know that everyone is looking forward to that. Aren't you?"

"Yes," Vicky agreed eagerly. After spending the evening with Mitchell's family, she was getting fond of the idea of being part of a large, and loud family. "I just don't think I'm what your mother would have expected."

"I hope not," Mitchell said with a chuckle. "My mother married me off when I was five to the neighbor's kid. Now, she's a champion monster truck driver and every time she sees me she wants to arm wrestle."

"Oh," Vicky tried not to laugh, but she couldn't help it, the laughter spilled out.

"See?" Mitchell said as he held her tighter.

"You're perfect for me, Vicky, nothing is ever going to change that," he kissed her firmly.

Vicky melted into his kiss. Her heart fluttered with the anticipation of becoming his wife.

"You better get home and get some rest," Vicky suggested. "Otherwise you're going to be too tired to enjoy your own bachelor party."

"Good point," Mitchell smiled and kissed her once more. "I'll see you in the morning."

"Good night," Vicky smiled at him as he stepped out of the kitchen and back towards the lobby. Vicky finished the last of the cleanup and then made her way into the lobby. Just as she was stepping into it, Sarah and her two sons burst through the front door. Sarah looked exhausted as she tried to herd the boys. Rory, who was three years old, was as energetic as ever. Ethan was six, and curious about everything, which meant of course that he had to touch everything in sight.

"Aunt Vicky!" they shouted at once as they spotted her. They both ran towards her. Vicky opened her arms to the boys and gave them both a tight hug.

"I'm so glad to see you both," she said happily. "Who wants to have a camp out in my living room?" she suggested.

"That sounds like a great idea," Sarah said.

Vicky unlocked the door to her apartment which was one side of the ground floor of the inn. Rory and Ethan burst past her to explore.

"Did you meet Mitchell's family?" Sarah asked as she stepped inside after her boys.

"Yes, we had dinner together," Vicky sighed. "They seem nice and a bit crazy. But I don't think I made a very good first impression."

"Oh, sweetie," Sarah said sympathetically. "I'm sure they loved you, but it doesn't even matter what they think, it matters what you and Mitchell feel for each other."

"Thanks," Vicky said as she gave her sister a light hug. It was exactly what Vicky needed to hear.

"Where's Aunt Ida?" Sarah asked as Vicky released her. As if on cue they heard the roar of a motorcycle outside the inn.

"Aha, she must have been out with Rex," Sarah giggled. "They're so cute together."

"Don't tell her that," Vicky warned. "She'll lecture you for hours about what is cute, and what is a mature sensual relationship."

"Oh no, thanks for the warning," Sarah laughed. Rex was a tall and burly biker who Ida had met and fallen hard for, though she didn't like to admit it. She now had her own motorcycle as well, but preferred to ride with Rex when she could. Vicky had warmed to Rex's relaxed attitude and she trusted him to keep her aunt safe, and even a little grounded.

"Hello, hello, I'm here," Ida said as she hurried through the door. "Sorry I'm late, things got a little hot and heavy," she winked. "If you know what I mean," she winked again.

"Yes, Aunt Ida," Vicky said. Sarah rolled her

eyes.

"We know exactly what you mean," Sarah assured her. "No need to give us the details."

"Let's make a pillow fort!" Vicky announced to the boys.

"I'll make some popcorn," Sarah offered and slipped away to the kitchen.

"I'll change into my jammies," Ida said.

The boys began racing around the apartment collecting pillows and piling them up. Soon the pillows had turned into a mountain in the middle of Vicky's living room floor. She giggled as she watched her nephews struggling to climb to the top.

"Hey, be careful!" Sarah chastised as she walked in with a large bowl of popcorn.

"They're doing great," Vicky laughed as she watched them climb.

"I'm telling you they must get that daredevil quality from their father," Sarah said as she shook her head.

"I don't think so," Vicky began to say. Before she could finish, they heard a wild shriek from the bedroom door. A split second later Ida launched herself onto the pile of pillows. She caught both boys in her arms and snuggled them close. They squealed as she covered their cheeks with kisses.

"You're right," Sarah grinned as she put the bowl down. "They take after their Great Aunt Ida."

"Ugh, great aunt?" Ida mumbled as she was struck by a flying pillow. "How about Fantastic Aunt Ida?"

The evening was perfect, and Vicky found herself feeling immensely grateful for the people in her life and the man she was about to marry. As she fell asleep that night, she forgot all about the disastrous dinner and instead felt the sweet anticipation of what was to come.

Chapter Three

Vicky's alarm went off early the next morning. She hurried to turn it off so that the boys wouldn't be woken up. She crept her way past Aunt Ida who was snoring on the couch. Rory and Ethan were curled up in their pile of pillows. She paused a moment as she wondered where Sarah was. Then she smelled the coffee brewing in the kitchen. Vicky smiled to herself. Sarah never missed a beat, and was always up and ready to go long before Vicky was.

"Here you go, bride-to-be," Sarah said as Vicky stepped into the kitchen. "We have a lot to do today," Sarah reminded her. "You're going to need plenty of fuel."

"I have to see Mitchell off first," Vicky said as she sipped the coffee. "Thank you for this," she added.

"Thank you for last night," Sarah said. "I haven't seen the boys have that much fun in a long time."

"I haven't had that much fun in a long time either," Vicky laughed. "Try and get a little you time in this morning before they wake up, hmm?"

"Oh no, no, my darling baby sister. This weekend is all about Vicky-time. So hurry up and send your man off to his wild bachelor party," she grinned.

"Some wild party," Vicky said with a roll of her eyes and a laugh. The group of men were spending the night camping and fishing at a beautiful spot by a river a couple of hours drive away. It was not exactly a traditional bachelor party, but Mitchell had very little interest in strippers. As Vicky stepped out into the lobby she noticed that Mitchell was already there, along with his father and brother.

"Do you have everything you need?" she asked. She was yawning when Mitchell spun around and tried to kiss her.

"Ugh, sorry," Vicky laughed.

"Oops," Mitchell smiled. "Everything I need, except for you," he said with a pout. "I don't want to go."

"Don't be such a wuss, Mitchell," Connor called out as he carried their bags out to the car. Mitchell shot a glare in his direction but didn't say anything.

"You're going to have a great time," Vicky promised him. "And so am I," she kissed him again, this time without the yawn.

"All right," he sighed. "Now, I'm not sure if the cell phone service has improved out there but the last time I went there was no service. So, if there are any problems, anything at all, just call me and I'll contact you when I can. Understand?" he met her eyes intently.

"I understand," Vicky replied. She laughed a little when Mitchell's expression was one of doubt.

"I'll be back tomorrow morning in plenty of time to get ready for the wedding," he smiled.

"Have fun," she insisted and nearly pushed him out the door. He was meeting up with Sheriff McDonnell, two other police officers, Rex, and Phil. Vicky was sure it was going to be quite an interesting experience for all of them.

Vicky watched as Mitchell drove down the driveway. As she was walking back to the front counter she heard the rumbling of a truck pulling into the parking lot. She peeked out the window, and just as she had hoped, it was a truck from Highland's Party Shop. It would have the party tent she had ordered. She was excited as she ran out the door to greet the delivery driver. A sullen young man climbed down out of the truck.

"Where do you want it?" he asked glumly. Vicky frowned at his attitude but she was determined not to sweat the small things.

"In the garden," Vicky pointed towards the aisle that had been created throughout the gardens just beyond the pool.

"Let me get my cart," the young man said and

walked around behind the truck. He opened the back doors of the truck and tugged down a metal cart. Then he reached into the truck and grabbed the tent which was in a long rectangular case. "Oof," he muttered as he pulled at the tent. "Did you order the deluxe or something?"

"Just the regular wedding tent," Vicky replied as she watched him struggle with the tent. She didn't think it should be that difficult. Then again from the redness of the boy's eyes and the way he kept swaying on his feet she was fairly certain that he was not completely sober. "Do you need some help?" she finally asked.

"No, I've got it," he replied gruffly and latched the tent to the cart. He wheeled it into the garden and placed it where Vicky asked. "Do you want me to help set it up?" he suggested as he glanced at her.

"No, I can set it up myself," Vicky said with confidence. The shop charged extra to set it up and she had used similar tents for celebrations before so she felt she could handle it easily.

Besides, she wasn't sure she would trust him to set up anything that her family and friends would be under.

"Suit yourself," he shrugged. He wheeled the cart back through the garden and loaded it back into the truck. As he drove out of the parking lot Vicky tried not to think about his sour attitude. She wanted to be excited over finally having the tent that she had been looking so forward to receiving. It brought home that the wedding was actually happening and it was very close.

"It's here!" she clapped her hands and started towards it.

As she hurried over to it, she heard someone call out from behind her.

"Don't touch it until I get there!" Ida hollered. Still dressed in plaid pajamas she rushed over to Vicky.

"Let's check it out," Vicky said happily. "But I think we should move it a few feet over there," she pointed towards the small fountain that had recently been installed.

"Perfect," Ida agreed. The two women grabbed the case containing the tent and tried to drag it over to the fountain.

"I didn't think it was supposed to be this heavy," Vicky grunted as she tugged at the end of the tent. Ida pulled as hard as she could, but the tent wasn't going anywhere. "On second thoughts maybe it's perfect right here," Vicky sighed.

"Good thing it was left in the right place," Ida said gleefully. It was in a beautiful spot in the center of the gardens. It was surrounded by blossoming bushes, and flowering trees. There would not even be a need to decorate the outside of the tent with flowers and ribbons, as nature was doing it for them.

"Yes, this will do just fine," Vicky nodded. "Well, I guess we better get it rolled out," she said.

"I can't believe you two are starting this without me," Sarah complained as she jogged over to them. "The boys are helping Henry make breakfast so I can help, too! I can't wait to see it up," Sarah grinned. "It's going to be perfect!"

The three worked together to roll out the tent. As they pushed Vicky still felt as if something wasn't quite right. They seemed so easy to set up when they were set up by the party shop and it had looked so much easier on the instructional video. Finally, the three gave it a hard shove, and the tent began to unroll all on its own.

"Now, that's more like it," Ida said and wiped her hands together. As the tent unraveled there was an odd lump in the center of it. Vicky's eyes grew wider as the tent spread out. The lump was still there.

"What's that?" she asked breathlessly as she began walking towards it.

"Maybe, it's just a place where the tent bunched up," Sarah said hopefully. Ida was staring at the lump with the same anxiety that Vicky was.

"A man-shaped lump?" she said with a shake

of her head. Vicky lifted the end of the tent and peered underneath. She gasped when she discovered what was hidden beneath it. She whipped back the tent to reveal the body of the new deputy sheriff, Arthur.

"Oh no!" Sarah cried out and covered her mouth with her hands.

"This can't be happening," Vicky groaned as she rushed closer to the body. It was clear that he was dead, and had been for some time, but Vicky still checked for a pulse, hoping that she might be able to save him. When she touched his skin it was cold. She knew that he was gone. She stared down at the body with disbelief. Not only was it the day before her wedding, but nearly the entire police force was off at a bachelor party.

Sarah dialed 9-1-1 and gave them the details.

Vicky stepped closer to him and tried to see how he might have died. His cell phone had fallen out of his pocket when the tent was unraveled. The touch screen was lit up so it must have touched something. She bent over to look at the phone without touching it. Displayed on the screen was a calendar reminder for an appointment at eleven-thirty the previous night. The appointment just said.

Meet PD

"PD," she repeated to herself. She wasn't sure what to think of the reminder, but perhaps this had something to do with Arthur's murder. Maybe it was a crime that could be wrapped up easily.

"We should call Mitchell," Sarah said as she stood beside Vicky.

"And Sheriff McDonnell," Ida agreed with a nod of her head.

Vicky was silent for a long moment and then looked up at the two women. She was about to speak up about her suspicions when it dawned on her just what was about to occur. In mere moments sirens would be blaring, lights would be flashing, and Mitchell's mother and sister would be witness to a murder investigation at the inn. If dinner didn't turn them off, she was quite certain a dead deputy sheriff would.

"Oh no," Vicky gasped out as she turned back towards the inn. "Mitchell's mother and sister will be awake soon. What if they see the police here? What if they find out about the murder?"

"Vicky, I'm sure that they will understand," Sarah said soothingly. "It's not like you had anything to do with this murder."

"No, they won't understand," Vicky said swiftly, her mind spinning with everything that was happening. "If we call Mitchell, he'll have to come back, he'll be busy with investigating the murder, and the wedding…"

"Vicky, listen to me," Sarah said sternly. "It's all going to work out, but you need to let Mitchell know what's happened. If you don't tell him someone else will and he'll be angry with you for not informing him." Vicky hated calling Mitchell back to deal with something like this, it might delay the wedding, and make it difficult for him to enjoy his time with his family. But she knew that she had no choice. Arthur's death had to be investigated.

"Fine," Vicky sighed and swept her hands over her face slowly. After she took a deep breath she looked between Sarah and Ida. She took her cell phone out of her pocket and dialed Mitchell's number. It went straight to voicemail. She was about to leave a message but didn't know what to say. She tried Sheriff McDonnell and it also went to voicemail. "They might already be out of range," she said after she hung up. "I'll call the local police station to tell them what has happened. The officers that stayed behind will just have to handle it until we can reach Mitchell and the Sheriff," Vicky said. "Besides, maybe it's not such a bad thing that we can't reach Mitchell."

"What do you mean?" Sarah asked and narrowed her eyes. "What are you thinking?"

"I'm just saying that Mitchell is only ever going to have one bachelor party. It is horrible what has happened to Arthur, but it's not going to hurt the case for Mitchell to be gone for one more day. Bobby and Norman can handle it."

"Bobby and Norman?" Ida asked incredulously. "Aren't they mainly crossing guards?"

"Sure, when there's nothing major happening," Vicky shrugged and tried to believe what she was saying. "I'm sure they went through the same training that Mitchell did. They should be able to handle this."

"Maybe," Sarah said thoughtfully.

"Bobby and Norman and the crime scene techs will have to handle it until Mitchell and the Sheriff can be contacted. If the murder isn't solved by the time Mitchell gets back, he'll just pick up where the other officers left off."

"I don't know," Ida shook her head slowly. "It feels like there's a lot more to this case than meets the eye. I mean he was wrapped up in your wedding tent, Vicky, what if the murder was a warning of some kind?"

"A warning to what, not get married?" Vicky frowned. "I'm not going to let someone bully me into being afraid."

"Let's not forget that it may have nothing to do with Vicky," Sarah pointed out.

"Well, we are just going to have to deal with the murder and organize the wedding," Ida stated.

Vicky sighed. "Maybe we should just postpone it. I don't see how it's going to happen now."

"Absolutely not," Sarah said and pursed her lips thoughtfully. "Okay, here's what we're going to do," Sarah said as she exhaled a long breath. "The boys are with Henry having breakfast. He can prepare breakfast for Maisy and Mae-Ellen as well. Then I'm going to take the boys, Mae-Ellen, and Maisy for a tour of the grounds and maybe I can convince them to go for a swim in the pool. I will just have to keep them away from this section of the grounds and that will give you some time to block off the area of the crime scene. We can just say it is blocked off because of the wedding, it's far enough from the main building anyway." Sarah held up her hands, "Just promise me that you and Aunt Ida won't get involved in the investigation"

"But Sarah..." Vicky began to argue.

"Thank you, Sarah," Ida said and shushed Vicky. Vicky sighed and tried to remind herself that a man had died, and that should be the focus of her thoughts. But her mind kept returning to her wedding. Once she had reported directly to the police station that there had been a murder, she knew that things were going to begin moving swiftly. She called the officer who she knew would be on duty, directly. She had got to know most of the officers at the station through Mitchell.

"Bobby, there's been a murder," Vicky said quietly into the phone.

"Ha ha, Vicky, very funny. I'll be sure to have

a good laugh with Mitchell about this when he gets back," he chuckled. Vicky frowned.

"Bobby, I'm serious, your new deputy sheriff, Arthur, is dead. I found his body in the rolled up wedding tent at the inn a few minutes ago. We have called the emergency number already, but can you try and come out here with as little fuss as possible. I have Mitchell's family staying here and I don't want to upset them."

"Yes, ma'am," Bobby replied without hesitation. He was always very obliging and tended to be quite good at following orders. Bobby was a good police officer for many things, but Mitchell had mentioned that he was gun shy, and he didn't handle confrontations well. Luckily, the murder took place before the tent was delivered and it's unlikely that the murderer would cause more trouble at the inn. Vicky hung up the phone and turned back to her aunt.

"So, what exactly are we going to do about all of this?" Ida asked as she placed her hands on her hips. "It doesn't look like he left any stains on the tent."

"Aunt Ida!" Vicky gasped reproachfully. "I think we should be focused more on the man who lost his life, not the party tent."

"It's sad," Ida agreed as she looked over at Arthur's body. "But let's be honest here, Vicky. We barely knew the man. For all we know he could be involved in criminal things, leading to his murder. What we do know is that your wedding is tomorrow, which means we have less than twenty four hours to figure out what really happened here, and fix it."

Vicky wanted to argue with her, but she couldn't. She knew that Ida was right. She didn't want her wedding to be ruined. She also wanted to make sure that Arthur's killer was brought to justice. She just hoped that both of these things would occur.

Chapter Four

Within minutes some officers including Bobby and Norman along with the EMTs had arrived. The medical examiner arrived shortly after the EMTs had confirmed that Arthur was dead.

"I'll go inside and check in with Sarah," Ida offered.

Vicky nodded and turned back to Bobby and Norman. The two stood back a few feet from the body, just staring at it.

"Your first?" Vicky asked gently.

"Yes," Bobby said.

"No," Norman replied. "But the first one that I shook hands with."

"I understand," Vicky nodded. "It's very hard to wrap your head around how someone can be alive and talking to you one minute and gone the next."

"It's not just that," Bobby frowned. "I can't even tell how this guy died. There's not a mark on him."

The medical examiner glanced up from the body. "It looks like suffocation. There's a bluish tint to his lips. Should I forward Sheriff McDonnell my report?"

"No," Vicky said automatically. The medical examiner looked at Vicky for a moment. He was fairly new to the town himself.

"I was asking the officers," he said pointedly.

"She's right," Bobby said quickly. "Sheriff McDonnell is out of the office and we can't contact him. Just send it to the main office. We'll take it from there."

The medical examiner looked a little concerned but he nodded. As he was taking care of the body, Bobby and Norman cornered off the crime scene as the crime scene technicians arrived.

While the technicians processed the scene,

Vicky led Bobby and Norman away from the garden. Vicky decided that in order for her wedding to go ahead she would need to assist the police to solve the murder as quickly as possible.

"Listen, I think the first step is to figure out why Arthur was killed," Vicky said quickly. "If you can figure out the motive then that will help you figure out who the murderer is. So, did Arthur mention anything to either of you about someone giving him a hard time? Did he have any arrests that were rougher than usual?"

"Well, Arthur had his first big bust already," Norman said as he scratched at his cheek.

"Yup, that was a pretty intense take down," Bobby nodded.

"Well," Vicky looked between both of them. "Do you think it's possible that the criminals that Arthur arrested had something to do with his death?"

Norman stared at her blankly. Then he nodded. "That's a good idea, Vicky. I hadn't even thought about that. In fact, they were released on bail yesterday."

"Do you know their names?" Vicky pressed and searched Norman's eyes for any sign of detective skills.

"I can look them up," Norman said and snapped his fingers. "There will be a record of it. I'll go to the station and do that now."

"I am going to stay here at the scene," Bobby assured her. "I'll make sure I don't mention dead bodies if anyone asks."

"Thanks," Vicky said with a small smile.

"I'll go find those details and I'll text them to you," Norman said to Bobby. "We'll get to the bottom of this," Norman said to Vicky with determination.

Vicky nodded. "Thank you," she said quietly. "Let me know if you manage to contact Mitchell or Sheriff McDonnell please."

"I will," Norman said with an eager smile. As Bobby walked towards the medical examiner and

Norman walked away, Vicky had to shake her head. She was sure that both men were more than capable of patrolling neighborhoods, manning crosswalks, and even nabbing shoplifters, but they were in way over their heads when it came to murder. She knew if this crime had any chance of being solved quickly she was going to have to play a part in it.

***

When Vicky entered the lobby she found Aunt Ida doing her best to entertain Maisy and Mae-Ellen.

"There are so many things to do in town," she was explaining. "In fact I'd highly recommend the Highland Museum, it tells a lot about the history of this town. There's even a little information about this house."

"Museums are fine," Maisy said with a frown. "But I'm more interested in something fun."

"Me too," Mae-Ellen said with a smile. "Vicky!" she waved to Vicky.

"Hi," Vicky replied with an awkward smile. "Did the two of you sleep okay last night?"

"We did," Maisy nodded. "I was hoping we'd see you at breakfast though."

"I'm sorry, I got tied up with some wedding business," Vicky attempted to explain.

"Maybe we could do lunch then?" Mae-Ellen suggested.

"Absolutely," Vicky agreed. Once Mae-Ellen and Maisy had headed off to their room, Vicky pulled Ida aside and spoke softly to her.

"Aunt Ida, I'm going to go to the party store to talk to Miriam," Vicky said. "Maybe she heard or saw something around the tent before it was delivered today."

"Okay," Ida nodded. "But be careful," she requested.

"I will, I promise," Vicky assured her. She

grabbed her purse and headed back towards the crime scene. She wanted to see if Bobby had received the information from Norman about the arrest. As she walked towards him he pulled out his phone.

"I just got the details," he said to Vicky as he looked at his phone.

"So young," she frowned as she looked over his shoulder at the names and photographs of the two young men who had been arrested. The charges were for drug possession and distribution. She wanted to ask Bobby if he could forward it onto her but she didn't want to press her luck.

"I'm going out now, but call me if you need anything," she called out to Bobby as she headed towards the parking lot.

As Vicky pulled out of the driveway she noticed that a dusty red car pulled into the road right behind her. The car drove casually behind Vicky, but Vicky felt compelled to repeatedly glance in the rearview mirror. She turned onto the main road that led into town. The car behind her turned onto the main road as well. Vicky sped up. She normally obeyed the speed limit fairly strictly, but she wanted to see if the car behind her would continue to keep pace. As she expected the car sped up as well. Vicky glared into the rearview mirror. She struggled to see if she could get a glimpse of who was driving. The sun was shining too brightly onto the windshield for her to be able to see. The party store was coming up on the right.

Vicky considered going around the block to see if the vehicle would continue to follow her, but she was more interested in talking to the shop owner. She assumed she was just being paranoid. But in case she wasn't, by parking she could get a look at the car's license plate when it drove past. She pulled into a parallel spot and turned in her seat to watch for the license plate. To her surprise the car suddenly turned off the main road and onto a residential road. It moved too quickly for Vicky to see the plate clearly. She could tell the make though.

Still a little uncertain of whether she was actually being followed or not, Vicky stepped out of her car and walked up the sidewalk to the party store. As she looked up at the shop she noticed that it was closed. She knocked lightly on the door and peered in through the window.

"Hello?" she called out. Through the window she saw a flicker of movement inside the shop. She knew that someone inside was checking to see who was standing outside. Vicky frowned as she wondered if they would open the door for her. Just when she was about to give up and walk away, the door unlocked and swung open. A tiny woman stood beyond it, her eyes puffy and red.

"Hi Vicky," she said nervously.

"Miriam," Vicky nodded softly. "May I come in?"

"Of course," she cleared her throat and stepped back so that Vicky could enter. The shop was dark with only one light on over the register.

Vicky glanced around the space, which in the shadows became downright eerie with all of the decorations and masks hanging from the shelves.

"I can't say how sorry I am, Vicky," Miriam gushed. "My lawyer says I shouldn't speak to you, but I just want you to know how sorry I am. I hope this isn't going to darken your wedding."

"Miriam, it's okay," Vicky said quickly and took Miriam's hands in her own. Vicky's hands engulfed the woman's delicate fingers. She could feel them trembling. "None of this was your fault," Vicky said softly. "I know it had to be as much of a shock to you as it was to us."

"I just can't understand it," Miriam shook her head and sniffled. "I don't know how this happened."

"Listen Miriam, does anyone have access to the party tents before they are delivered?" Vicky asked.

Miriam stared at her for a long moment. She seemed to be considering how to answer the question. She lowered her eyes.

"I'm not really supposed to talk about the case."

"Oh, Miriam, don't be silly I'm not going to sue you," Vicky said with a shake of her head. "You don't need to worry about it."

"It's not about that," Miriam said, her eyes widening slightly. "You don't know, do you?"

"Know what?" Vicky asked with confusion.

"I think that you should go, Vicky," Miriam said and gestured to the door. "It's not a good idea for you to be here."

"I don't understand, Miriam, what don't I know?" Vicky asked.

Just then the door swung open and Vicky turned to face one of the prime suspects in Arthur's murder. Only then did she make the connection between the last names. Smith was such a common surname that she hadn't realized Josh Smith and Miriam Smith were related. Not only that, Josh had been the sullen delivery driver that had dropped off the extra heavy tent at the inn.

"You," Vicky gasped out, too surprised to say something more intelligent.

"Mom?" Josh asked. "Why is she here?"

"I'm sorry, Josh, I just wanted to apologize to her..." Miriam attempted to explain through tears.

"For what?" Josh demanded as he stepped further inside. He pushed the door closed behind him and turned the lock on the door. Vicky felt her heart begin to race. She stepped a little closer to Miriam, whether to protect her, or protect herself, she wasn't sure. Josh's expression grew even angrier as he glared at Vicky.

"You might as well just sign my confession for me, Mom," he said snidely. He looked to be in his late teens. "I told you I didn't do it," he growled at his mother. "Why don't you believe me? You're my mother, you should believe me!"

"What am I supposed to think?" Miriam cried out. "First you're arrested for drugs, drugs!" she shook her head and sobbed. "Now this?"

"You're supposed to know that I'm not a killer!" Josh cried out with frustration. Vicky moved between Miriam and Josh. She could tell that things might get out of hand, and quickly.

"Josh, just calm down," Vicky insisted as she tried to meet his eyes.

"How am I supposed to calm down when the fiancée of a Highland PD detective is questioning my mother against my wishes?" Josh demanded, his voice growing louder with every word he spoke.

"Hey Josh, I'm just here to talk with your mother. It's all right," Vicky insisted. "If you say you didn't do it, then tell me where you were last night after you got released on bail?"

He frowned and stared hard at the floor. "I can't," he said quietly.

"Josh, tell her the truth," Miriam pleaded. "You say you didn't do this, but you won't tell me where you were last night and I know you weren't home."

Josh squeezed his eyes shut and shook his head slowly back and forth.

"Josh, what is it?" Vicky pressed. She felt like he wasn't trying to hide something out of fear, he was hiding it out of shame.

"I don't want to say," he frowned and shoved his hands into his pockets. "If I tell the truth I'm going to be in even more trouble."

"More than murder?" Vicky asked.

"I didn't kill that cop," Josh nearly shouted. "I had nothing to do with it. There's no proof that I did, because I wasn't there, I didn't kill him. If I did, why would I wrap him up in one of the shop's tents?" he demanded. "What would be the point of that?"

Vicky frowned. He made a good point. Why would he murder someone and then not even bother to try to conceal his involvement. He would have to expect to be one of the first people that the police would investigate.

"Then where were you, Josh?" Vicky asked again. "If you tell the truth, Josh, you're not going to have anything to worry about."

"Fine," he finally sighed. "The truth is, Pat and I went to get high. Okay? We were at a drug den in North Jessup. We were there all night."

"Josh," Miriam gasped out with disgust and disappointment. "You just got out on bail!"

"I know, Ma," Josh rolled his eyes. "You see?" Josh demanded and shook his head. "That's why I didn't want to tell you. I knew you would look at me like that. Besides, who is going to believe a druggie?"

"Oh, Josh," Miriam wiped at her eyes. "I just don't know where I went wrong."

Vicky frowned. She had no doubt that Josh was telling the truth.

"Whatever, Mom," Josh said with a sharp shake of his head and unlocked the door. He slammed his way through it, causing the door to bang closed behind him.

"I'm sorry, Vicky," Miriam said with a sigh. "I just don't know what to do."

"It's all right," Vicky replied calmly as she stared out through the door after Josh. Maybe Josh wasn't a killer, but he sure was traveling down a hard road.

"I remember when he thought the sun rose and set with me," Miriam said sadly and wiped at her eyes.

"It looks like he still thinks that, Miriam," Vicky touched the woman's shoulder gently. "He was so afraid to disappoint you that he was willing to be accused of murder, Miriam. I think maybe he still needs you much more than you think."

"Maybe so," Miriam agreed with a soft smile. "Well, with the shop closing I'll have more time to focus on his recovery."

"You're closing?" Vicky asked with surprise.

"I think it's for the best," Miriam said quietly. "I should get back to packing."

Vicky frowned as she watched Miriam walk

towards the back of the shop. She was sure that there was more to this than met the eye. Why had the killer gone to so much trouble to make sure that Arthur's body ended up right in the party tent? She left the party shop and decided to head into the police station to discuss what she had learned about Josh with the officers. She didn't want them wasting time chasing down a lead that would lead nowhere.

Chapter Five

When Vicky arrived at the station there was a bit of a commotion near the front desk. A woman in a sleek, red dress with her thick, black hair pulled up into a messy bun at the back of her neck, was slamming her hand hard on the desk as she glared at Bobby.

"Where is the sheriff?" the woman demanded. "My husband has been murdered. Who is in charge here?"

"Uh well," Bobby stared at her with wide eyes. "He's..."

"Away at the moment," Vicky supplied as she stepped up beside the woman. "I'm so sorry for your loss," she added with genuine sympathy.

"Thank you," the woman stuttered as she looked from Bobby to Vicky. "But I really need to speak with the detective investigating this matter."

"Of course you do," Vicky nodded. "I'm Vicky by the way."

"Poppy," she said.

"I'll be back in a minute to help you," Bobby said. "I've just got an important call to take."

"Is there anything I can help you with?" Vicky offered as Bobby walked away. "I'm engaged to Detective Mitchell Slate and I know everyone here, so if you have questions I might be able to get them answered for you."

"Oh," Poppy frowned. "Well, I just want to know what's happening with the investigation."

"I'm sure Bobby will fill you in when he comes back," Vicky said. "Why don't we take a seat while you wait for him," she added. "Do you have any idea who would have wanted to kill Arthur," Vicky asked gently as they walked over to the wooden bench.

"No," she said as she shook her head.

"Did Arthur have any arguments with anyone since you moved to Highland?"

"No, not really," Poppy shook her head again and then gazed steadily at the floor. "I mean, other than me. It was like we couldn't stop fighting after we came here. Arthur kept complaining about how boring the town was," her voice caught as she took a sharp breath. "He kept saying how there was no danger here, no reason for him to even put on his uniform. But if I even brought up the idea of moving, he became furious."

Poppy and Vicky fell into an awkward silence at that statement. It was clear that Highland had not been a safe place for Arthur.

"Was there anything in particular that he didn't like?" Vicky asked. "Maybe someone giving him a hard time?"

"No, he didn't have a problem with anyone that I knew of," Poppy shrugged. "But I'm sure there was something bothering him."

"What do you mean?" Vicky asked.

"He was just very aggravated. He kept looking

out the windows, kept insisting that I not give out our new address, all of this weird stuff," she shook her head. "He could be such a weirdo."

Vicky frowned but kept her thoughts to herself. It seemed odd to her that Poppy was not more upset about the untimely demise of her husband. Perhaps she was in a state of shock.

"What about back home?" Vicky suggested casually. "Did he have any enemies that might have followed him here?"

"I don't think so," Poppy shook her head. "Arthur wasn't the type to make enemies. He was always more bark than bite," she explained.

"I see," Vicky nodded as she sat back against the bench. She noticed that Poppy seemed remarkably comfortable talking about Arthur. She didn't compliment him, or seem to be grieving the loss of him. Nothing she mentioned was followed by any emotional response other than disdain.

"Was he a good husband?" Vicky asked softly.

"You can tell me, I know what it's like to be in a relationship with a police officer," she explained, hoping that Poppy would feel comfortable enough to confide in her.

"He was a husband," Poppy shrugged mildly. "He did what he was supposed to do, no more no less. The trash was taken out, the bills were paid, and he ate the dinners I cooked."

"Well, that sounds nice," Vicky offered hesitantly. It was as if Poppy had just rattled off a shopping list rather than a description.

"Nice is one way to put it," Poppy agreed and then cast a dismissive gaze in Vicky's direction. "I know that you're engaged, but have you ever been married before?"

"No," Vicky said softly.

"Well, I wish I could say that I recommend it," Poppy said with a slight laugh. Vicky frowned as Poppy stood up from the bench.

"If you need anything please don't hesitate to let me know, okay?" Vicky honestly wanted to support the woman but she was also hoping she might reveal some information to her that might help solve the murder.

"Okay," Poppy nodded and clutched at her purse. "But I doubt I will."

"I just need to ask you a few questions," Bobby said as he walked over to Poppy.

"About what," she asked.

"Where you were last night."

"Why?" Poppy asked defensively.

"Just so we can get a picture of what Arthur was doing before the murder," Bobby explained as casually as he could. "Was he home with you? Were you out? Were you home alone?"

Poppy shook her head and muttered under her breath. "I knew it. It's always the spouse right?" she asked as she looked from Bobby to Vicky. Vicky shook her head slowly.

"I wouldn't say that," Bobby said. "But every detail is important and can help solve the murder."

"Well, there's nothing to tell," Poppy said in a harsh tone. "I was home alone for most of the night. Arthur left and then didn't come home again, I thought he didn't come back because he was upset, but obviously there was a different reason."

"I'll need your official statement," Bobby said. "It won't take long," he assured her.

"Okay," she finally relented and followed Bobby over to his desk. Vicky walked over to Norman who was flipping through a filing cabinet.

"Have you heard from the medical examiner about the official time of death?" she asked.

Norman nodded. "He places it at about midnight last night. He also said that Arthur was likely suffocated by a plastic bag of some kind. There's no bruising on his face, so he doesn't think someone pressed on his nose or mouth."

"So, it had to be someone strong enough to

subdue him," Vicky said with a frown.

"Or someone he felt no danger with," Norman pointed out.

Vicky thought about the reminder on his cell phone that was scheduled for eleven thirty in the evening. That was around his estimated time of death. Could PD mean police department? It was possible but that didn't quite fit for her, as it wasn't worded as she would expect it to be. However, Arthur wouldn't have feared a police officer. He might have thought he was safe with the person.

"Were there any calls for police around the time of Arthur's death?" Vicky asked.

Norman shook his head. "It was a very quiet day, as usual."

"PD," Vicky repeated to herself. "It must mean something." Just then Poppy and Bobby returned.

"Thank you, Poppy," Bobby said as he nodded to the woman. Poppy turned and quickly walked out of the building.

"Poppy," Vicky said softly to herself and then turned to Norman. "Norman, can you find out what Poppy's maiden name is?" Vicky asked. "Perhaps she's the PD on the phone."

"She doesn't look strong enough to take down a man like Arthur," Norman said with disbelief. "And why would he have a reminder to meet with his wife."

"I know but let's not get caught up with that right now. I think it's important to consider she might be a suspect. Poppy isn't exactly a devastated widow."

"I know, but people react in different ways," he said thoughtfully. "It can't hurt to look into their finances and see if there might be some kind of motive for her to kill her husband."

"Great idea," Vicky agreed. Norman was turning out to be more competent than she originally thought.

"On it," Norman nodded sternly.

He headed off to check on the details of Poppy's past and their financial records.

Chapter Six

Vicky decided that she would take a walk around town and see if anyone had been looking for Arthur. If PD was someone from his past, they would probably ask around town about him. She first spent a little time driving up and down the main strip of town. She was watching for that dusty red car that had seemed to be following her earlier in the day. She didn't notice that, but she did see Poppy knocking on the window of the party shop. She looked pretty annoyed as she waited for someone to open it. Vicky watched from her car. Miriam finally opened the door of the shop. She did not open it far enough for Poppy to get inside. The two women spoke tensely for a moment, then Poppy began swinging her arms with frustration. Vicky rolled down her window so that she could hear the exchange.

"I want my paycheck," Poppy was saying loudly.

"I'm sorry, Poppy, we already mailed it out," Miriam said quickly. "After you quit, we didn't think you would want to pick it up, so we just mailed it off to you."

"Sure," Poppy said, obviously irritated. "Because why bother to do the courteous thing and walk next door to hand it to me."

"After what happened, I thought it would be best if we didn't have a lot of contact," Miriam shot back.

"It was just a silly argument," Poppy said glumly. "It's not my fault that my husband walked in on your son in the middle of a drug deal."

"Shh," Miriam demanded sharply. "I don't want any more bad information about my family getting out in this town."

"Is it bad information if it's the truth?" Poppy asked impatiently. "Your son deserved to go to jail for what he was doing. Don't think I don't know that my husband ended up dead wrapped up in one of your party tents. It was probably your little hoodlum that did it."

"He has an alibi," Miriam snapped.

"Do you?" Poppy asked as she glared at the woman. "Maybe you took overprotective parenting to the next level?" she suggested. "Was it revenge for your son being arrested, is that why my husband needed to die?"

Vicky was about to climb out of her car to intervene, when Miriam ducked back into the store and closed the door. She left Poppy staring at her own reflection. Vicky didn't want Poppy to know that she had overheard the entire argument, so she slid down low in the car seat. After a few moments Poppy shook her head and stormed off.

Vicky was left with the mystifying task of adding Miriam, a sweet woman who she never would have suspected, to her list of potential murderers. After waiting a few minutes, Vicky climbed out of her car and walked towards the diner across the street from the party shop. If she was looking for someone, she would always check at the cheapest eatery in town first. Inevitably people who are new to town or passing through, end up at the diner.

When Vicky opened the door she found that the diner was relatively empty. Maude was behind the counter. She had only started working there recently since her husband had passed away because she found it too boring to stay home alone. She had her silvery blonde hair in spikes along the top of her head. She had colored the tips of the spikes bright pink.

"Vicky," she said as she looked up at her. "I didn't think I'd see you in here today. Shouldn't you be with your aunt, getting ready for your wedding?"

Maude was a good friend of Ida's, and they tended to try to outdo each other with their fashion sense and hairstyles.

"Don't worry, it's still on," Vicky said with a slight laugh. "Actually, I came in to see you. I was wondering if you'd noticed anyone asking around for the new deputy sheriff."

"The one that was killed?" Maude gasped. Vicky raised an eyebrow at how fast information traveled in a small town. She just hoped that by some miracle Mitchell's family hadn't found out yet.

"Yes," Vicky nodded.

Maude looked thoughtful for a moment and then nodded slightly. "Actually there was a fellow in here just the other day. In fact he even left me his card, in case I saw Arthur. Of course I knew exactly where Arthur was, but I wasn't about to tell a stranger that."

"Do you still have his card?" Vicky asked hopefully.

"I believe I do," Maude said as she rummaged on the shelf beneath the register. "Here it is!" she announced and handed it over to Vicky. Vicky stared down at the business card. It only had a name on it along with a telephone number. There was no description of what business the man,

Peter Palumder, might be in.

"Thank you, Maude, this is very helpful," Vicky said.

"Is Mitchell back yet?" Maude asked. "Did he come back to work on the case?"

"No, not yet, we can't get hold of him," Vicky said quickly. "Bye Maude!" she waved and walked out of the restaurant. As soon as she walked out of the restaurant, she called Norman.

"I just wanted to let you know that apparently a guy named Peter Palumder was asking about Arthur in the past few days."

"I'll see what I can find out about him," Norman replied. "Straight away."

Vicky could hear his fingers flying across the keys.

"I'm sorry, did you say his name was Peter Palumder?" Norman asked with surprise in his voice.

"Yes, it is," Vicky replied, as she walked over

to her car and unlocked it. She squinted in both directions down the street, watching for the red vehicle.

"You think he might have had something to do with Arthur's death?" Norman asked nervously.

"Maybe," Vicky replied. "Have you found out something about him?"

"There's a warrant out for his arrest for suspicion of loan sharking, and previous charges of assault," he replied with displeasure. "Vicky, you need to stay away from this guy. He could be dangerous."

"He's a loan shark?" Vicky asked with surprise. "Well, that makes sense I guess," she shook her head. "He must have followed Arthur here."

"Are you all right?" Norman asked. "You're not with him now are you?"

"No, I'm not," Vicky said. "I'm fine."

"I'll get his description and information out to

everyone on patrol and see if we can snag this guy before he disappears," Norman said. "Be careful please. Mitchell will kill me if you get hurt," Norman said anxiously.

"I'll be fine, Norman," she promised him and hung up the phone before she could be questioned further. As she drove back to the inn, Vicky kept her eyes peeled. She was willing to bet that the red car she had seen belonged to the loan shark. If he had killed Arthur, that might mean that he had yet to get the money he was looking for, which could mean that Poppy was in danger.

***

When Vicky arrived at the inn she found Ida attempting to play badminton with Mae-Ellen and Maisy. Every time she lunged to swing the racket she nearly fell into the net. Vicky was surprised at first, as she was sure Ida was much more agile than that. Then she noticed Ida's spiked heels sinking into the ground.

"Aunt Ida, what are you wearing?" Vicky laughed as she walked up to her.

"I'm trying to break them in for the wedding," Ida explained with a huff.

"Hi again, Vicky," Mae-Ellen waved to her. "I feel like I've seen you for all of about five minutes today."

"Hi," Vicky said with a guilty frown. "I'm sorry, there's just some last minute running around I have to get done for the wedding."

"It's okay," Mae-Ellen replied. "I'm worn out from the game. Let's go get a cold drink, Maisy," she suggested. Once the two women had walked away, Aunt Ida stepped closer to Vicky.

"Did you find out anything about the case?" she asked hopefully.

"A man, Peter Palumder, has been looking for Arthur. When Norman looked him up, he found out that Peter is wanted for loan sharking."

"A loan shark?" Ida asked with amazement. "You don't want to mess around with those types."

"Yes, I know," Vicky nodded. "But this also means that Arthur must have been up to his ears in debt. Poppy never mentioned a loan shark hounding them."

"Funny that Poppy didn't mention that when you spoke with her," Ida said with a light cluck of her tongue. "I think we should talk to her again."

"Yes, I think so," Vicky nodded.

"And I think you both need to stay out of it," Sarah snapped from just behind them. Vicky and Ida looked over at her guiltily. "In case you two haven't noticed, I'm still trying to run an inn here," she said sharply. "I've got two little boys running around, guests demanding my attention, and a wedding that I am apparently putting together all by myself. Meanwhile, two of my very favorite people in the world are actively trying to get themselves in the middle of a dangerous investigation. Do you think that maybe you could consider backing off the murder mystery and helping me out with some of this? I know you want to help solve this, Vicky, but you have to stay out of it like I said, especially if it puts your life in danger. You've got to think about how Mitchell would feel if he found out you were hurt in any way while he was gone."

Vicky grimaced guiltily. She knew that Sarah was right. Sarah had sent her husband off on the bachelor trip on the understanding that Vicky and Aunt Ida would be around to help with the boys. Now, she was juggling everything herself. But she also knew that there was no way she could stay out of the investigation, now. She really wanted it solved so her wedding could go ahead without a hitch. She would just have to make sure she helped Sarah more and didn't neglect her own wedding.

"Are the boys done with their video games?" Vicky asked innocently. "I bought them a brand new one to play."

"Right, and about that video game that you

left them in front of hours ago, Vicky, they have ratings on them for a reason!" she huffed.

"Oh dear," Ida cringed. "I might have overlooked that when I picked it out."

Vicky and Ida exchanged worried glances before looking up at Sarah's annoyed expression.

"How about we take the boys for ice cream?" Vicky suggested. "Then we could drop them off at that play gym for an hour or so, and we can come back here and focus on setting up for the wedding. Does that sound good?" Vicky asked hopefully.

"Actually," Sarah sighed with relief and nodded. "That sounds like a great idea."

The three women walked into the lobby of the inn. Vicky noticed that there were quite a few guests milling about. She hadn't realized that Sarah had so much to contend with. Rory and Ethan were playing tag with one of the bellboys right in the middle of the lobby.

"Boys, Aunt Ida and Aunt Vicky are taking you for ice cream!" Sarah called out. Instantly, two wild-eyed and exuberant little boys came barreling towards Ida and Vicky.

"Ice cream, ice cream," they chanted. Sarah smiled smugly as she looked over their heads at her sister and aunt.

"Have fun," she said gleefully and hurried away to tend to the guests. Vicky looked at Ida. Ida looked back at Vicky. Then they both looked at the little boys.

"Ice cream, ice cream," they both began chanting with a laugh. As they left the inn and headed towards Vicky's car Vicky noticed the dusty old red car parked in the parking lot. She glanced at Ida.

"Get the boys settled in their seats. I'm going to go check out that car," she said.

"Okay," Ida nodded and eyed the car seat and booster seat. "Right..." she hesitated and looked at the two little boys. "You can tell me how these things work, right?" she asked hopefully.

The boys laughed as they climbed into the car.

As Vicky began walking across the parking lot towards the car she felt a little nervous. She had never seen the car parked before. The fact that it was parked directly in the parking lot of the inn made her think that the driver was being quite bold. Of course she still could be paranoid about being followed by the driver of the car. But she was not going to pass up getting the license plate and peering inside to see if there was anything interesting.

Vicky was a few feet away from the car when a figure suddenly sat up in the driver's seat. Until that moment she had assumed that no one was in the car. The shock of seeing someone sit up was magnified by the shock of hearing the engine roar to life. She glanced back over at Ida who was still struggling to get the boys in their car seats. Vicky's heart began to pound heavily as she looked back at the driver. Once more the sun glaring on the windshield was keeping her from seeing any specific details about the driver's face. But what she did see was the car moving directly and swiftly in her direction, and beyond her, in the direction of her car, Ida, and her young nephews.

"Stop!" Vicky cried as she raised her hands in front of her. She knew that she was no match for a vehicle, but she would try to be if it meant protecting her family. She cringed as she expected the car to slam right into her. Then she heard the popping sound of gravel spitting out from under the tires. The car turned in the other direction and squealed out of the parking lot. Vicky stared after it, too shocked to think to look at the license plate. She was just relieved that no one had been hurt. She looked over at Ida who had jumped at the sound of the squealing car.

"Are you okay?" Ida asked as she looked back at Vicky.

"Yes," Vicky replied. "Are you?"

"Yes," Ida nodded. Then she peered into the car. "But I might need a little help."

Vicky walked over to the car and looked into the backseat. She raised an eyebrow at the way Ida had used the seatbelts to literally tie her great nephews into their seats.

"Help us, Aunt Vicky," Ethan said with a giggle.

"Oh yes, I will," Vicky laughed. "If your mother saw this...," she grinned at Ida.

"I tried!" Ida said and stomped her foot.

Vicky couldn't help but giggle. Ida had never had children of her own, and though she had been involved in her and her sister's lives growing up, she was never really around long enough to learn about things like car seats and safety issues. Vicky on the other hand had been well educated by both Sarah and her brother-in-law about the proper use of car seats. That didn't mean it was easy for her either, though. Once she finally got them buckled safely into their seats she closed the door. She stood beside the car and spoke quietly to Ida so that the boys could not hear.

"I'm pretty sure that was a warning," Vicky said grimly. "I think we might be getting close to the truth."

"Too close," Ida said with some concern. "And with the kids with us we need to be more careful."

"I agree," Vicky nodded. "But we also need to find out the truth. It's the only way we can be sure that we'll all be safe."

"I think we better head out to Poppy's to see what she has to say as soon as possible," Ida said. "Let's take care of the boys like we promised and then get back to the investigation."

Chapter Seven

When Vicky and Aunt Ida arrived with the boys at the ice cream shop, Vicky kept a watchful eye out for the car. She had just begun to relax a little when she noticed it through the glass window of the ice cream shop. It was driving quickly down the main road towards the larger plots and farmland that surrounded Highland. She nearly bolted up out of her chair.

"What is it, Vicky?" Ida asked and caught her ice cream just before it would have tipped onto the floor.

"It's the car," Vicky said. "We should follow it!"

"Vicky," Ida said reproachfully. "The kids," she tilted her head towards the two little boys who were covered in ice cream and chocolate syrup.

"Oh right," Vicky pursed her lips. She knew she couldn't take off after the car but she needed to solve the murder mystery quickly. "Hurry up, boys," she said. "If you eat your ice cream really fast I'll give you each a cookie!"

Ida laughed and shook her head. "I used to do the same thing to you girls. Your parents were not too happy about it though," she cringed.

Rory and Ethan gulped down the remainder of their ice cream. While Vicky cleaned them up, Ida paid for two cookies. As they were walking out of the ice cream shop, Vicky watched for any sign of the car.

"Vicky, I've been looking everywhere for you!" Mae-Ellen said as she walked up to them.

"Oh Mae-Ellen, I'm sorry, we were supposed to have lunch weren't we?" Vicky asked guiltily.

"Yes," Mae-Ellen replied with a frown. Then she looked down at the two boys. "Oh, aren't they just darling!" she said happily. She reached out to ruffle their hair. When she pulled her hand away from Rory's head she had a good amount of chocolate syrup smeared across her palm. "And sticky," she muttered.

"So, sorry," Vicky said and handed her a tissue.

Mae-Ellen wiped her hand clean. "What are you doing out on the town when there's a wedding to organize?" she asked with concern. "You're not having second thoughts are you?" she narrowed her eyes intently.

"No, absolutely not," Vicky said quickly. "We just wanted the boys to have a little fun, since weddings can be so boring for kids, you know."

"Sure," Mae-Ellen nodded. "So, then you're heading back to the inn?"

"Actually, we promised to take these two to the play gym for a few hours," Ida explained. "That way we can get some work done on the wedding."

"Oh good," Mae-Ellen smiled. "I'll expect to see you back at the inn in time for a late lunch then, Vicky?" Mae-Ellen posed her words as a question, but Vicky could tell that they weren't actually a question.

"We'll be there," Vicky assured her. "In the meantime, if you need anything, you can always ask Sarah."

"Mmhm, your sister has already been there to help me quite a bit," Mae-Ellen said with some disdain. "I guess she's used to taking care of things for you."

Ida raised an eyebrow. "They help each other," Ida said firmly.

"Well, you certainly helped her kids to enough sugar," Mae-Ellen laughed as the boys began chowing down on their large chocolate chip cookies. Vicky felt as if Mae-Ellen's laughter was not a sign of amusement.

"I'm really sorry, Mae-Ellen, we're late getting them to the play gym, but I'll see you soon," Vicky said as her heart dropped. She was beginning to believe that her future mother-in-law really did not like her one bit.

"I'll be waiting," Mae-Ellen said with a dramatic sigh. Then she walked past Vicky and down the sidewalk towards the inn. Vicky frowned as she looked over her shoulder at the woman.

"Don't let it get to you," Ida warned her. "She's just a mama tiger looking out for her son."

"I am not interested in seeing her claws," Vicky sighed and helped the boys into the car.

"Well, hopefully they will pick up that loan shark and get to the bottom of all of this," Ida said glumly. "Do you think he was the one driving the car?"

"It makes sense to me," Vicky nodded her head. "I don't know why he would be following us, though."

"Maybe Poppy will be able to answer some questions for us," Ida said as they drove to the play gym. Stepping inside the play gym was like stepping into the loudest baby toy ever invented. There were flashing lights, blaring music, and vibrant colors in every direction. It made Vicky's head spin.

"Hi Ethan, hi Rory," the overly cheerful woman behind the counter cried out. She was wearing a clown nose and had her hair up in pigtails. She had to be in her twenties, but she looked like she was dressed for kindergarten. Vicky forced a smile.

"They're just going to stay for a few hours," Vicky explained.

"Oh, I know," the woman said perkily. "I spoke to Sarah. Everyone is so excited about your wedding, Vicky!"

"Thank you," Vicky said as she watched the two boys take off into the play area. "We'll be back soon to get them."

"Take your time, there must be so much to do!" the woman said gleefully before she chased after Vicky's nephews.

"She's right you know," Ida said as she opened the door for Vicky. "There is a lot to do. We can't ignore the wedding altogether."

"I'm not sure that there will be a wedding if

we don't figure this out," Vicky said with a frown. "I wish that I could get a hold of Mitchell and Sheriff McDonnell."

"I know, Vicky," Ida agreed. "It would probably hurry things along if they could help with the investigation."

"Are you the one who sent the cops after me?" a harsh voice demanded as they stepped out onto the sidewalk. Vicky jumped back slightly as an angry face came into view.

"Who are you?" Vicky was startled.

"Peter Palumder," he replied. Vicky tensed, she was not sure if he was the killer, but he was a loan shark, which immediately made Vicky very wary of him.

"Lower your voice," Ida commanded him and gestured for them both to step away from the entrance of the play gym.

"You two have it all wrong if you think I had anything to do with the murder," Peter said sharply, but he stepped away from the door.

"Was it just a coincidence that you were looking for Arthur on the same day that he ended up dead?" Vicky asked trying to sound more inquisitive than accusative.

"Yes, it was," Peter growled. "Yes, of course I was here to find Arthur," he took a deep breath and shook his head. "Look, Arthur made some bad investments," Peter explained as he glanced from Vicky to Ida. "He knew what he was doing when he borrowed the money, and he knew what the consequences would be if he couldn't pay it back."

"Death?" Vicky prompted and took a step closer to Peter.

"Death?" Peter repeated and glared at Vicky. "I don't kill people. Dead people don't pay interest."

"So, maybe you tried to collect. Maybe you heard about the inheritance…" Vicky started to suggest, but Peter interrupted her.

"All right, I did," Peter admitted. He frowned

as he glanced over his shoulder and then looked back to the two of them. "I heard about the money, and I wanted a piece of it. That's my job. I came here to have a discussion with him," he added, emphasizing the word discussion.

"Maybe the discussion didn't go well," Vicky suggested. "Maybe Arthur tried to fight back."

"Arthur would never fight me. I didn't have to lay a finger on him. He knew what was at risk, if he didn't pay, I would reveal his illegal activities to his superiors and ruin his career. That man loved his job, he wasn't going to risk it."

"So, what did happen when you talked to him?" Vicky pressed.

"That's the thing, I didn't talk to him," Peter said with exasperation. "I was looking for him when the news spread that he was dead. Then when I tried to leave today, I saw I was being hunted down at the airport. There were flyers with my face on at every ticket counter."

Vicky raised an eyebrow, she was impressed

with the initiative that Bobby and Norman had taken.

"I knew if they caught me, then I would have no chance. I'll be locked up before I even have the chance to tell my side. I overheard one of the officers at the airport saying something about Vicky being the one to give him the information. So, I started to ask around, and it wasn't hard, because everyone is talking about the amazing wedding between Vicky and the newest Highland Police Department detective. So, I'm here to tell you, I didn't do this."

"Why would you come to me?" Vicky asked. "What do you think I can do?"

"Because you can help me prove I had nothing to do with the murder," Peter growled.

"How can I possibly do that?" Vicky enquired.

"Because I was a guest at your inn," Peter replied sharply. "And I was there all night."

"Really?" Vicky's eyes widened. She didn't remember seeing him at the inn but she had been preoccupied.

"Check your cameras," he insisted. "I went back to the inn after I left Arthur's house. I had quite an interesting discussion with his wife by the way."

"Poppy?" Vicky asked. "You spoke to her?"

"She never mentioned that, did she?" Ida asked and narrowed her eyes suspiciously.

"She is a very angry woman," Peter said with wide eyes. "When I told her I needed to talk to her about Arthur's debts she threatened to kill me herself. I told her I didn't want any trouble, just the cash, and gave her my business card so that she could have Arthur call me. Then I went back to the inn, where I stayed. Imagine my surprise when I saw the police activity this morning, and now I can't get out of this town!"

"Well, that has nothing to do with me," Vicky said. "This is a police matter."

"So, you're not going to help me?" he asked desperately.

"I can't," Vicky replied. "You need to speak with the police."

"We can help with that," Norman said as he stepped out from behind Peter. Vicky had slipped her hand into her purse and texted Norman the moment that Peter had confronted them. Norman had parked his squad car further down the block and then walked up to them silently.

"Come on, really?" Peter pleaded as Norman ushered him towards his squad car. "I didn't do this, Vicky. Check your cameras, and you will see."

"Quiet," Norman demanded. "I'm just taking you down to the station for questioning," he explained. "Are you ladies okay?" Norman asked as he looked between the two women.

"Yes," Vicky replied. "Will you let us know if he confesses or you arrest him?"

"Will do," Norman said before hauling Peter off to his car.

As soon as Norman and Peter were gone, Vicky and Ida hopped into the car and they headed straight for Poppy's property.

"I can't believe Poppy never said anything about a loan shark looking for Arthur," Vicky said as she drove along the country road. "That seems suspicious to me."

"Think of it this way," Ida said with a frown. "She had just inherited a property and there was already a loan shark sniffing around wanting to take it right from her. She must have been livid that Arthur's financial problems had followed her here."

"Financial problems that she never bothered to mention," Vicky pointed out.

Chapter Eight

As Vicky and Ida pulled onto the road that led to Poppy's property, Vicky squinted to see if she could spot a car in the driveway. Vicky had only been out that way once before, when Miriam had put the party tents and jumping castles on display at her property so she could take photos of them for a brochure. She had invited Vicky to have a look at them once they were set up since she was often using them for weddings and other events. Miriam's family property was adjacent to the one that Poppy had inherited. She noticed that there was a for sale sign in their front yard. Not only were they closing the shop, but they were also selling their property. That was surprising to Vicky.

"Looks like someone's home," Ida said as she tilted her head towards a car parked in the driveway. Vicky was relieved to see that it wasn't the car that had been following them. It was a tiny convertible that looked like it must have cost quite a bit. Vicky parked beside it and the two women stepped out of the car. There was a light on in the three-story house. It wasn't a mansion by any means, just a large, old house with plenty of repairs that needed to be done.

When Vicky made her way up the steps to the front door, she heard music playing inside. It was quite lively for a widow in mourning. She exchanged a glance with Ida who nodded her head a little. Vicky knocked on the door loud enough to be heard over the music. After another set of knocks, Poppy opened the door. She was dressed in a tube top and tiny jean shorts. Vicky found herself instantly falling into the judging trap, as Poppy was in her forties, certainly not some teenage girl to be wearing such revealing clothing. She tried to push the thought from her mind as even Aunt Ida had recently worn a tube top.

"How can I help you?" she asked. Her body was covered with a thin sheen of sweat.

"Could we come in for a moment?" Ida asked

as she met the woman's eyes.

"Oh sure, yeah," Poppy nodded and held the door open for them. As the two stepped inside, the music became even louder. Poppy bounced across the living room and turned the radio off. Vicky could see why she was sweating. There were boxes everywhere. Poppy must have been packing up the contents of the house.

"What's going on?" Poppy asked as she turned back to the two women.

"Just thought we'd pop by and see if you need anything," Vicky said casually.

"Thank you, I'm fine," Poppy said with a smile. "I've been busy getting this place packed up so I can place it on the market."

"You're selling it?" Ida asked as she began to casually walk around the living room.

"Yes, I don't want to stay here by myself," she sighed.

"Do you need help with the funeral arrangements?" Vicky asked gently.

"The medical examiner refuses to release the body. Says, that until the investigating officer releases it, he can't guarantee me when I can have it. Which means I can't make arrangements yet," Poppy explained.

"Well, hopefully they'll wrap it up soon," Vicky offered. "I just ran into Peter Palumder," Vicky added nonchalantly.

"Oh, you did?" Poppy asked as she frowned. Vicky noticed her nervously fiddling with a bracelet that hung from her wrist.

"He mentioned that he met with you the day Arthur was killed," Vicky said. "You didn't mention that when I spoke to you before."

Poppy sighed as she looked between the two of them. "I didn't think it was important."

"Surely, a loan shark showing up on your door step the day before your husband was found dead is relevant," Ida pressed as she turned back to look at Poppy.

"'I should have said something," Poppy said

with a concerned look. "But I didn't want anyone knowing a loan shark was chasing me for money. I was embarrassed I guess."

"And we wanted to let you know that Peter was just taken into custody," Ida said gently. "So, whatever his involvement with you and Arthur is will probably be revealed."

"Look, I had nothing to do with this," Poppy said with exasperation. She looked truly flustered. "Peter can reveal everything now, it makes no difference. It's not like it will implicate me in the murder. Peter showed up at the door talking about a debt I never even knew that Arthur had. I told him I had nothing to do with it, that it was between him and Arthur, and I had no idea where Arthur was. He threatened me, he said as far as he was concerned Arthur's debt was my debt, and if we didn't come up with a way to pay it then he was going to start breaking fingers. Can you imagine? I thought they only did that sort of thing on television," she shook her head with disgust. "It's horrible the things that Arthur got into. Look, it's no secret that we weren't in some hot love affair, but Arthur used to be a decent man. I don't know what happened that made him get involved in the things he did, but whatever it was, had nothing to do with me. Now he's gone, I can't change that, and you can't fault me for not collapsing in grief. It isn't my fault that he put himself in danger."

Poppy's words rung clear through Vicky's mind. She wondered if she was really taking a risk she shouldn't be by involving herself in the case. She was after all actively placing herself in danger. If Mitchell knew about her activities, he wouldn't be surprised, but he wouldn't be happy. They weren't even married yet, and he would know that she would try to solve the murder.

"Wait, you said you didn't know where Arthur was, but did you have any idea who he might have been with?" Vicky suddenly asked.

"No, if I did, I would have told the police that. That night we had a big fight about the house. I wanted to sell it, he didn't. Maybe he was afraid it would draw Peter's attention, but like I said I didn't know about any of that. He was off sulking, playing on his phone, then all of a sudden he said he had to meet someone and took off out the door," she shook her head. "He never made any good choices, not a single one."

"Hopefully, Peter will tell the same story that you just did," Vicky said. "By the way, what were you and Miriam arguing about at the party shop today?" Vicky asked gently. The question surprised Poppy. She stared at Vicky for a moment. She looked as if she was deciding how to answer the question.

"When we first moved here I decided to pick up a little part-time job so that I could have an excuse to be out of the house. I heard Miriam was hiring for the season so I applied and got the job. I was only there for a few hours and I noticed that Josh was up to something. When Arthur picked me up, I mentioned it to him, and Arthur went to talk to him about it. He caught Josh and his friend in the middle of a drug deal and arrested them both on the spot. Miriam blamed me for her son going to jail and started shouting. I quit on the spot. I still wanted to get paid for the few hours I worked as it's not my fault that her son is a drug dealer. In fact, if they're looking for a murderer, they should look at Miriam Smith."

"Miriam," Vicky said with disbelief, she still couldn't imagine Miriam murdering anyone.

"Now, if you don't mind, I need to get back to work on packing. As soon as I can sell this place, I'm going to. There's a property developer interested, I'm sure he's going to want it."

"Good luck," Ida said and turned back towards the door. Vicky followed after her.

"Do you think it could have been Miriam?" Vicky asked once they were outside.

"Maybe, or maybe Poppy just wants us to think it's her," Ida said thoughtfully. "That way she could get rid of both of her problems in one shot. She could get rid of her husband and get revenge on Miriam for losing her temper and for losing her job."

"Maybe," Vicky said as they reached the car.

As soon as they were in the car again, Vicky let out a growl of frustration.

"I just don't understand. None of this makes sense. There are plenty of people who could have done it, but none of them seem like the right fit. What do you think?" she glanced over at Ida.

Ida was staring out the window at something. She didn't answer Vicky.

"Aunt Ida?" Vicky asked again and leaned forward to try to see what Ida was looking at. Not far down the road, in the driveway of Miriam's property, a dusty red car was idling. "It's the car," Vicky gasped. "Maybe we can finally get the plate!"

She started the car and gunned the engine.

"Be careful, Vicky," Ida warned. The driver of the car must have noticed that they had been spotted. It zoomed down the driveway in reverse. It spun out on the old country road and then sped off down the road. Vicky pulled out behind it and sped after it. The potholes in the old untended road made the ride feel like an out of control roller coaster.

"Vicky, watch out!" Ida cried out when the driver in front of them suddenly hit the brakes. Vicky had to slam on her brakes to keep from sliding into the back of the car. The driver in front of them took a hard right and sped off down the road. Vicky was too breathless to drive after him. Once she surfaced from her shock, she started to turn in the same direction.

"No," Ida said sharply. "Don't Vicky," she reached out and put her hand on the steering wheel as well.

"What do you mean?" Vicky demanded. "He's going to get away."

"One more second and we would have crashed into the back end of that car," Ida pointed out. "We're not going to take another risk like that, not with your wedding so soon."

"Aunt Ida," Vicky sighed as she stared after

the car which was now only a dot in the distance. "That might have been our only chance to solve the murder."

"I'm sure it wasn't," Ida said and rolled her eyes. "Don't be so dramatic, dear."

Vicky stared at her aunt with disbelief. She found it hard to believe that Ida could accuse anyone else of being dramatic.

"Vicky, you're not thinking clearly," Ida said with mounting concern. "You have to take a breath and calm down before you lose control of this situation. You have a lot on your mind from the wedding to Mitchell's family being here. I know that you can figure this out if you just find a way to clear your mind."

"You're right," Vicky nodded slowly and took a deep breath. "I've never been so stressed. This was supposed to be a nice time for me to get ready for my wedding, and instead I'm frustrated and confused. I'm pretty sure that Mitchell's family hates me."

"First of all, they don't even know you," Ida reminded her. "They haven't had the chance to get to know you. Secondly, even if they do hate you, it's their loss, now isn't it?" Ida asked. "You need to stop worrying about impressing them so much. Just be yourself. Part of you is an amazing sleuth, and that's the part we need right now. Because, as far as I can tell we're at a dead end."

"I know," Vicky said and rested her forehead briefly against the steering wheel.

"But there must be something. There must be some clue that will give us an idea of who exactly he was meeting with. Who PD actually is. If the cameras prove that Peter is telling the truth about being at the inn all night, then there must have been someone else. I don't think that Poppy is lying about him taking off to meet with someone, otherwise he would have been there when Peter arrived. I remember when I first met Arthur, he was so paranoid, he kept looking around at everyone and everything. It makes sense now that I know he had a loan shark after him. What I don't understand is who he would just take off to meet in the middle of the night. He didn't know anyone in Highland as far as I know. So, who was he going to meet?"

"Maybe it was another debt collector," Ida suggested. "Peter might not have been the only one who was on the hunt for him."

"That's a good point," Vicky nodded. "If only there was a way to know for sure who he was meeting with around the time he was murdered," she paused a moment and stared out through the windshield. Luckily there wasn't a lot of traffic on the country roads so no one was blaring their horn behind the car. She felt as if she had the first quiet moment to think. "Wait a minute!" she gasped out. "Poppy said that he was playing on his phone. Maybe whoever he met with called or texted him about the meeting. If so we might have a record of who the last person was that saw him alive."

"Don't you think that Bobby would have checked that out?" Ida asked incredulously. "That should have been the first thing that they checked."

"Maybe," Vicky shrugged.

"Well, let's go by the station and see if they did," Ida suggested.

"Yes," Vicky nodded. She started to drive down the road. As she drove she went over the clues in her mind. She knew that most of them had been ruled out by circumstance and general disbelief, but there was one key point that she hadn't thought much of since ruling out Miriam's son as a suspect. Arthur's body had been wrapped up in a party tent. He hadn't just been tossed in a ditch somewhere. He had been deliberately placed in a party tent. The only reason that Vicky could think of that someone would be that specific in the disposal of a body, was because that person wanted to make it look like Miriam or someone from her family was involved.

The discovery of the body inside of the tent was likely to put a big dampener on their sales. But the fact that her son was accused of the murder would have made it difficult if not impossible for her to continue to run a business in the small town of Highland. Even though he had been ruled out as the murderer, that suspicion would always hang over the family's reputation. By the time she reached the police station, her mind was buzzing with who might gain something from Miriam's shop closing.

"Vicky, are we going in?" Ida asked after Vicky had parked in front of the police station.

"Oh yes," Vicky nodded. "Let's see if they found out any more information from Peter."

Chapter Nine

The moment Vicky and Ida stepped into the police station, Vicky regretted it. She heard Maisy's southern drawl all the way from the front door.

"Bobby?" Vicky asked as she walked up to the front desk. "What is going on here?"

Bobby was grinning from ear to ear as he turned to look at Vicky. "Maisy was just telling us some stories about our detective Mitchell from when he was a little too young to wear a badge."

"Maisy?" Vicky asked as she stared over at the woman who was seated at Norman's desk.

"Oh Vicky, I was wondering where you were. I got bored at the inn so I decided to come down here and take a look at where my brother works," she smiled charmingly at Vicky.

"In the middle of an active..." Vicky halted before she could finish her sentence. She was about to reveal what was really going on, and then remembered that she didn't want Mitchell's family to find out.

"Bobby, Norman, can I speak with you please?" Vicky asked.

"I'll keep an eye on Maisy for you," Ida said with a glimmer in her eyes. Vicky knew that she just wanted to see the baby pictures of Mitchell. But it would be easier to talk with Bobby and Norman if she wasn't distracted by Ida.

"Absolutely," Norman stood up quickly. He and Bobby stepped out from around the front desk and lined up in front of Vicky. "How can we help?" Norman asked.

"Did you interview Peter?" she asked as she looked between the two of them.

"Yes," Bobby nodded.

"Did he give you any new information?" Vicky asked hopefully.

"No," Norman replied with a slight shake of his head.

"And his alibi?" Vicky asked.

"We confirmed it," Norman said. "We released him about ten minutes ago."

"You released him?" Vicky asked with wide eyes. "But he was the main suspect..."

"Not with an alibi he wasn't," Bobby pointed out.

"What about Arthur's cell phone?" Vicky pressed. "Did you recover it?"

"Yes we did," Norman nodded. "Why?"

"Did you check it to see who the last person that contacted Arthur was?" Vicky asked.

"The computer tech is looking into it," Norman said. "I'll see if he knows who it is yet."

"Thanks," Vicky said appreciatively. "We need to figure out what happened to Arthur, and quickly. His wife is planning on selling the property and leaving town as soon as Arthur's body is released. I still have a feeling she's involved in this somehow. As for Maisy," Vicky said as she lowered her voice even further. "Please make sure that you don't mention the murder to her."

"Oh, are you kidding?" Norman laughed. "She has baby pictures!"

Vicky looked up at Maisy, who was grinning. "Oh boy, I hope that Mitchell doesn't find out about this," Vicky said but she couldn't help but laugh a little. Maisy seemed to be quite happy to share as much as she could about Mitchell. While Vicky waited for Norman to check into the phone, she leaned back against the front desk. She heard Bobby on the phone.

"I just want to confirm that it is Poppy Darcy?" he asked. "Thanks," he hung up the phone.

"Poppy's maiden name is Darcy?" Vicky asked as she looked back over at Bobby.

"Yes," Bobby nodded. "Looks like she might be our PD after all."

"Maybe," Vicky nodded slowly. Something

just didn't feel right. Was it possible that Peter and Poppy had been in on the crime together? "Norman, the phone?" she called out. Norman had been drawn back into the baby picture fest that was occurring around Maisy.

"The tech says the last call was to a number that wasn't on his contacts list. It was a little before eleven at night."

"Were they able to find a name connected to the number?" Vicky asked hopefully.

"It's a private listing," Norman shrugged. Vicky knew that Mitchell had ways of getting information that the rookies were not privy to.

"I've got the number here. I'll try calling it," Norman said. He went behind the desk and called the number.

Then he hung up.

"It was the voicemail for Stan Vincont, a Property Developer," Norman explained to Bobby as Vicky listened closely.

"Arthur called a property developer just

before his murder," she shook her head slightly. Then it began to dawn on her. Poppy and Arthur had been arguing about selling the property. Meet with PD likely stood for property developer. Maybe Arthur had made a plan to meet with Stan Vincont and decline his offer to purchase the house. Maybe Poppy had found out about it and she had killed Arthur.

"Aunt Ida," Vicky gestured to the woman who was fully enraptured in an image of Mitchell on the back of a stuffed horse with a lollipop tucked behind his ear.

"Vicky, you have to see this," Ida said with a laugh as she held up the picture. Vicky stared at the picture. She wanted to stay focused on the crime, and solving it. But those adorable blue eyes made her heart melt.

"He was so cute," Vicky gushed.

"Cute, and a terror," Maisy corrected her. "That boy had a temper. He still does. If you do anything to cross him, he never lets you forget it," she shook her head with a smirk.

Vicky frowned. Maisy's words sunk in. Was she doing something that crossed a line with Mitchell? Would he be able to forgive her for investigating the case without his knowledge? It wasn't like she hadn't looked into cases before and besides he couldn't be contacted, she thought, trying to justify her actions and calming her nerves.

Vicky took out her phone and searched the internet for an address for Stan Vincont. She could find a home address but no business address. The address was in a neighboring town so that was why she hadn't heard of him before.

"Maisy, we'll see you later?" she asked and raised an eyebrow.

"No rush," Maisy laughed. "I'm having a great time."

"Ready?" Ida asked as she stepped up beside Vicky.

"Don't you think that we should do something

to stop her?" Vicky asked with a grim frown.

"It's a little late for that now," Ida said with a laugh. "Besides, it will be a nice little surprise for Mitchell to come back to after the honeymoon."

"Good point," Vicky couldn't help but laugh a little.

"I've got an address we need to check out," she said. "Let's get moving before we have to pick up the boys."

"All right," Ida agreed. As they piled back into Vicky's car, she caught a glimpse of Maisy leaving the police station. She had her very own souvenir badge and had managed to snatch one of the officer's hats. Vicky couldn't help but notice how much she looked like her brother. She smiled to herself at the thought of adding another sister to her family. She was looking forward to getting to know Maisy and Mae-Ellen, she just hoped that she would have the chance to.

***

It took Vicky and Ida about half an hour to reach Stan Vincont's home address. The house was a modest rancher. The yard was well-tended with an assortment of flowers blooming in a small garden. There was a square placard hanging from the front door that advertised his services as a property developer. Vicky and Ida walked up to the front door.

"It doesn't look like he's home," Ida said as she peered into the front window of the house.

"No car in the driveway," Vicky observed as she studied the empty driveway.

"No lights on inside," Ida said. "Do you want to knock?"

"No, let's take a look around back," Vicky said as she was already halfway around the house.

"Vicky, someone might see us," Ida warned as she followed after her.

"Like who?" Vicky asked as she rounded the back of the house.

"Like him," Ida said when over the fence she spotted a mountain of a man in the neighboring house watering his garden. He turned off the hose when he saw the two women.

"What are you doing back here?" he asked in an aggressive tone.

"We're just looking for Stan," Vicky said quickly. "We were supposed to meet with him about a property."

"Well, you just missed him," he said as he tilted his head towards the front of his house. "I saw him leave about ten minutes ago, that's why I came back here to water. I try not to disturb him if he's home."

"Oh darn," Vicky pouted. "I knew I didn't get the time right for our appointment. Any idea where he might be?"

"Uh well," the man squinted into the mid-day sun. "My best guess would be out on the old Darcy property. That's all he's been talking about. He has this grand plan with the Darcy and Smith properties."

"A grand plan?" Vicky asked curiously.

"I probably already said too much," he shook his head. "It's never going to work out anyway. The woman that inherited the property isn't going to sell. At least, last I heard."

"Thanks, you've helped us out a lot," Vicky said and Ida offered him a warm smile.

"No problem," he said and turned his hose back on. He hummed softly as he watered the plants. Vicky and Ida walked back towards the car.

"That confirms it, Stan might just be the last person who saw Arthur alive. He might be able to give us some information," Vicky said hopefully. "I think this is our last chance of getting this murder solved before tomorrow morning when Mitchell gets back."

"I think you're right," Ida said as she glanced at her watch.

Vicky drove above the speed limit as she

headed towards Poppy's house once more. She parked a few houses down from Poppy's property so that they wouldn't alert her to their presence. She hadn't been too friendly on their last visit. As they walked up to the property from the rear, they could hear voices. Vicky tugged Ida behind a large shed so that they could listen in.

"You're not just playing with me again, are you, Poppy?" a male voice asked.

"I'm serious this time," Poppy replied. "Now there's nothing to stop me."

Vicky stole a glance around the side of the shed. She saw a man who looked to be in his late forties or early fifties. He was wearing a black suit. In his hand he held a clipboard. He had his back to Vicky, but she could clearly see Poppy.

"It's Poppy and I bet that's Stan," Vicky hissed to Ida.

"Shh, let's listen to what they're saying," Ida said and leaned closer to the edge of the shed.

"Look, my husband was the one who didn't

want to sell. Now he's dead, and has left me all of his debts. I have a loan shark after me. If you want this place, it's yours. But you have to pay me fast," she crossed her arms and looked at him sternly.

"Well, Poppy I'm sure that we can work something out to make that happen," he said as he adjusted his thin brimmed hat. "As I said, I am very interested in the house and the land. Would you be willing to sign something today?"

"I would," she nodded quickly. "Let me just give my lawyer a call, and see if he can meet us."

"Sure," he nodded with a slight smile. "It's always good to have all your ducks in a row."

Poppy looked at him strangely for a moment, and then stepped into the house.

"Look at that," Vicky said with a slight smirk. "I bet it was Poppy who killed her husband after all."

"What makes you think that?" Ida asked as she watched the man walking casually across the side yard of the property.

"Think about it. Poppy inherited this house and this land. It was hers. But Arthur was insisting on not selling it, probably because he was scared that the loan shark would take that money from him and that Poppy would find out about his debts. Or maybe because he wanted to wait until it was worth more. Either way he was standing between her and a lot of money. She probably decided she'd had enough and got him out of the way."

"Hmm, not exactly a happy marriage," Ida said with a sigh.

"Not in the least," Vicky agreed. "Poppy made that clear with the way she talked about him, like he was just a piece of furniture that she had to live with."

"Years go by," Ida pointed out. "Some marriages end up that way."

"Not mine," Vicky said with confidence. "If I ever start feeling that way about my marriage, I'll do something about it."

Ida offered her a tolerant smile as if she knew a little more about life than she did, but she did not press the matter. "Well, why don't we ask that fellow a few questions? Maybe Poppy let something slip about how she killed her husband."

"Maybe," Vicky agreed, still a little troubled by the look that Ida had given her. As they slipped out from behind the shed, Vicky kept one eye on the porch of the house to watch for Poppy.

"Hello there," Ida said as she walked up to the man. He glanced down at his clipboard, and then up at Ida. He took a slight step back when he saw her.

"What are you doing here?" he asked.

"We're interested in this property," Ida explained smoothly. Vicky stepped up on the other side of the man. She watched the way he clutched nervously at his clipboard.

"It's not for sale," Stan said sharply as he eyed the two.

"Why not?" Ida asked. "I heard it was."

"I'm already buying it," Stan explained.

"Maybe we could make the owner an offer," Vicky suggested. "I heard her husband just recently passed. This place must have some bad memories."

"What do you know about that?" Stan asked with some interest.

"About Arthur being murdered?" Ida asked. "Well, it's all over town."

"Too bad they haven't arrested the killer yet," Vicky sighed.

"Did you know Arthur?" Ida asked.

"We met once or twice," he replied and shook his head. "It's a shame what happened."

"Well, I bet Poppy will be looking to sell quickly," Ida said. "I wouldn't want to live in a town where my husband was murdered."

"That makes sense," Stan nodded.

"Stan, did you meet with Arthur before his

murder?" Vicky asked boldly.

"What?" Stan stammered out.

"Do you know anything about the murder?" she asked.

"Like what?" Stan asked, and then lowered his voice. "What exactly do you want to know?"

"I just want to know if Arthur mentioned fearing for his life, or whether his wife had been threatening him," Vicky explained.

Stan stared at her for a long moment.

"Actually, I do have something that might interest you," Stan said and tilted his head towards the driveway. "If you want to take a look it's in my car. When I heard about the murder I was a little unsettled by it, so I decided to keep it. I guess," he hesitated a moment and lowered his voice, "I was hoping to settle things with Poppy first."

"We'd like to see it now, please," Vicky said and crossed her arms with disdain.

"It's right over here," Stan explained. As they walked towards the driveway, Vicky whispered to Ida.

"Looks like we'll finally have some proof we can use. Maybe they'll be able to arrest Poppy and we'll have all of this wrapped up before Sarah even misses us."

"I don't think so," Ida said as she slowed to a stop.

"Huh?" Vicky asked and then turned to look ahead of her. Parked in the driveway was the dusty red car. Vicky looked from it, to the man who was standing beside the car.

"It's in the trunk," he explained and popped the trunk. Vicky stood frozen with fear as she stared at the man. She had suspected that the man who had killed Arthur was the same person who had been driving the car. Did that mean that Stan was the killer?

"Well, then you should just drive it down to the station," Vicky suddenly said. "We're not police officers after all."

"I know that," Stan said in a darker tone. From under the clipboard he was holding he produced a gun. He must have drawn it while they were walking to the car. Now he was wielding it with complete confidence. "I do my best not to get involved with law enforcement, but sometimes they just happen to get in the way. You two ladies however, don't have badges, do you?" he smirked. "So, I think we'll be just fine."

He pointed his gun in the direction of the trunk. "Hop in please," he said.

Vicky looked over at Ida. She knew that if she screamed, Poppy would hear her. But what would Stan do if Poppy came running out of the house? Would he shoot her on the spot? Would he shoot them? It was too much of a risk to scream.

"In the trunk," Stan repeated and took a step closer to Ida. "If either of you scream, I will shoot."

"You first, Vicky," Ida said as she gritted her

teeth. Vicky knew that Ida was trying to decide whether she could successfully knock the gun out of Stan's hand. Her aunt had more up her sleeve than just a strange fashion sense, she was also a black belt, she had taken down many foes. Vicky was nervous that her aunt might make a mistake however and get herself shot.

"No, Aunt Ida," Vicky said sharply. "You first."

Ida glared at her with frustration.

"Get in the trunk!" Stan barked and released the safety on the gun.

Vicky cringed and stepped towards the trunk. Ida glared at Stan, but since he had the gun trained on Vicky she wasn't going to take any chances by attacking him. Vicky stood nervously beside the trunk. It was empty inside, and actually quite roomy, which she was grateful for. But she had to wonder if it would end up being her coffin. She reluctantly climbed inside. Ida climbed in after her. Once the two were in the trunk, Stan produced a roll of duct tape. He tore off a length of it and handed it to Vicky.

"Put it on," he instructed as he gestured towards her mouth, and then did the same to Ida. Vicky put the tape lightly over her mouth. Stan reached down and smoothed it tight across her mouth. Vicky's eyes widened at the sensation of not being able to breathe through her mouth. He did the same to Ida.

"Turn over," he instructed.

Vicky and Ida managed to wiggle onto their stomachs.

"Hands behind your backs," he commanded.

Reluctantly, both women complied with the request. Stan grabbed Vicky's hands roughly and crossed them behind her back. He wrapped duct tape around them. When he grabbed Ida's hands she kicked her feet wildly and flailed in an attempt to escape him. She was grunting behind the tape that covered her mouth. Stan waved the gun in front of her face so that she could see it. Ida was instantly still. Stan taped Ida's hands and then slammed the trunk closed.

Chapter Ten

Vicky and Ida were immersed in darkness. Ida began mumbling, though the tape prevented her from actually speaking. Vicky tried kicking at the trunk. Ida squealed and shook her head, indicating that Vicky should stop. Vicky stopped, and soon realized that if Stan heard them kicking he'd open the trunk and tape their legs too. She was very still as she heard voices outside the trunk.

"My lawyer gave me confirmation over the phone," Poppy explained. "I can sign anything you need. If we can get this done today, that would be great."

"Perfect," Stan said and the voices began to fade away. Vicky could only assume that the pair were walking away from the car. She gritted her teeth. She wanted to bang on the trunk to alert Poppy, but she didn't want to put the woman at risk. She also wasn't entirely convinced that

Poppy was not in some way involved. Ida grunted quietly and began squirming in the trunk.

Vicky huffed as Ida kicked her square in the back. The sharp heel of her shoe was certain to have left a mark. Vicky's eyes widened at the thought. She wriggled around until she had the point of Ida's heel against the duct tape on her hands. Ida got the idea that Vicky was trying to convey. She stuck her foot out straight while Vicky pushed the tape hard against the heel. It took a few tries but finally she felt the heel push through. She wriggled the tape back and forth on the heel until enough of it ripped that she could pull her hands apart.

Immediately Vicky reached up to her mouth and tore the duct tape free. She had to bite her tongue to keep from screaming in pain as the tape pulled at her skin. She twisted in the trunk until she found Ida's hands. She released them from the duct tape. Ida tugged at the tape on her mouth but was much gentler about removing it. Once the two women were free, Vicky reached into her pocket for her cell phone. She knew there wasn't time to call for help. If Stan came back and found them unbound in the trunk he wasn't going to hesitate to shoot them. What they needed to do was get out of the trunk. Vicky turned on her phone and used it as a flashlight.

"Vicky, are you okay?" Ida asked when she finally got the tape off her mouth.

"I think so, are you?" Vicky asked as she glanced over at her.

"I'm fine," Ida replied. "But I'd be better if you had taken the hint and gotten in the trunk first so that I could attack that little punk..."

"Aunt Ida," Vicky said with a groan. "Let's just get out of here, then we can argue."

"There should be a release somewhere," Ida said as she felt around her side of the trunk.

"If it has one," Vicky said with a grimace. She swept the light from her phone around the underside of the trunk closest to the back seat. She noticed a small black lever. "I think I have found it," Vicky said and reached for the lever.

"Vicky wait," Ida hissed. There were voices outside the trunk.

"I just have to get one last paper," Stan was explaining. "It'll only take a minute."

"Okay let's just get it wrapped up," Poppy insisted. "I can't wait to leave this place behind. Can you believe that the local police actually had the nerve to practically accuse me of my own husband's murder?"

"What a shame," Stan replied. "That must have been very offensive."

"It was," Poppy replied. "Maybe Arthur and I didn't always see eye to eye, but I didn't want him dead."

"I'm sorry for your loss," Stan replied. "It's quite tragic."

Vicky felt sick to her stomach as she listened to Stan expressing sympathy to the woman he had made a widow. Now she knew that Poppy wasn't involved, but that didn't make anything better.

Stan was going to have to get rid of them to keep them quiet.

"Here it is," Stan said and Vicky heard a car door slam shut. This time the voices did not fade away. Vicky had no way of knowing if Stan and Poppy had gone back inside, or if Poppy was signing the paper on the trunk of the car.

"What do you think, Aunt Ida?" she asked as she shone her cell phone in her aunt's direction.

"Once the car starts moving, we lose our chance to escape," Ida said. "If we get out now, we might be able to escape before he even notices we're gone."

"If he's not just outside the car," Vicky whispered back.

"It's our only chance," Ida replied. "Go ahead, try the lever."

Vicky reached out and grasped the lever. She said a silent apology to Mitchell, just in case she didn't make it to the wedding, then she tugged the lever. The trunk latch released. With a gentle shove Ida pushed the trunk open a few inches. Both women waited a moment, to see if the trunk would be thrown open. Then Ida pushed it open enough that they could fit through. Vicky looked out through the opening. She didn't see anyone nearby. But the front door to the house was wide open. Vicky put her finger to her lips and Ida nodded.

Carefully, they climbed out of the trunk. Vicky crouched down low, hoping not to be spotted by anyone inside the house. Then she grabbed Ida's hand and started to tug her away from the car. Ida leaned slowly on the trunk. She pressed it down until it latched closed. Then she let Vicky lead her to the shed. They ducked down behind it. Vicky called the emergency police line while Ida kept watch on the house. Vicky was making the report when she heard the engine roar to life. She knew that Stan was driving away.

"Poppy," Vicky hissed. "I hope she's okay."

"I can see her on the porch," Ida said quickly. "She's all right, but Stan is getting away!"

"Should we chase him?" Vicky suggested.

"Do you have a gun?" Ida asked with a shake of her head.

Vicky frowned. "I gave a description of the vehicle to the dispatcher. Hopefully they will catch him before he gets too far."

"Well, at least the murder is solved," Ida said. "There's no question that Stan is the killer."

As they stepped out from behind the shed, Poppy spotted them. She hurried down the front porch and across the driveway towards them.

"What are you doing here?" she demanded. Her eyes lingered on the duct tape that still clung to one of Vicky's wrists. "What's going on?"

"Stan murdered your husband," Vicky said as she tugged the duct tape off her wrist. "We just escaped from the trunk of his car."

"What?" Poppy gasped. "Let me call for help," she said quickly.

"We've already done that," Vicky said. "For

now, you should stay safe in your home. If you see Stan's car, just dial the emergency number."

"I will," Poppy agreed.

"Hurry Vicky, we need to get to the police station," Ida said and grabbed her hand. The two ran the distance to Vicky's car. Vicky drove swiftly down the road. She could see a few patrol cars zipping down the road in the opposite direction. She hoped that they were onto Stan. But there was another concern that was rising in her mind.

"What if he goes to the inn?" she blurted out as she took a hard right. "What if he goes after Sarah or the boys?"

"Gun it," Ida commanded her. Vicky did as she was told, and the car roared down the road in the direction of the inn. She had never driven so fast before. When she skidded into the parking lot the tires kicked up quite a bit of gravel. As Vicky rushed from the car towards the entrance of the inn, Ida followed after her, still hobbling in her heels. Vicky lunged through the door of the lobby.

"Sarah?" she called out desperately. "Rory, Ethan?" she yelled. Vicky's heart dropped as she realized that she had forgotten all about the boys being at the play gym.

"Vicky," Sarah said with ice in her eyes as she walked out of the restaurant towards her. "Did you forget about something?"

Vicky looked over at her guiltily, but before she could defend herself, two more voices chimed in from the stairs.

"Vicky!" Mitchell's mother and sister cried out.

Vicky lowered her head. Every time someone said her name it set her nerves on edge.

"Vicky," Henry called out from the doorway that led to the kitchen.

"Wait! Please! Everyone!" Vicky growled. "There is a murderer on the loose, and we all need to make sure that everyone is safe!"

"Is that so?" Mitchell asked as he sauntered into the lobby from the restaurant. "Vicky?"

"I'm sorry!" Vicky announced and waved her hands in the air. "I'm sorry, Sarah, I should never have left the boys at the play gym. I'm sorry, Mitchell, I shouldn't have looked into the murder by myself. Most of all I'm sorry, Mae-Ellen and Maisy, that you haven't gotten to experience what the Heavenly Highland Inn is really like because I've been too busy trying to hide all of this from you. But now we have to keep an eye out for this man," she pulled up a photograph of Stan on her phone that she had asked Bobby to send through and showed it to everyone. "If you see him, don't speak to him, just call..."

"Me?" Mitchell supplied and took the phone out of Vicky's hand.

"What are you doing home?" Vicky asked as she looked into his eyes.

"I came home because Bobby managed to contact me and let me know that the deputy sheriff had been murdered," he stated.

Vicky stared at him for a moment, then she

turned to Sarah. "Sarah, the boys?" she asked. "Are they okay?

"Vicky, they are fine," Sarah said with a slight frown. "The play gym has my number, and they called me when you didn't pick the boys up."

"I'm so sorry," Vicky murmured. "I just got caught up in all of this. We couldn't get hold of you and I thought I could handle it and..."

"Shh," Mitchell said and hugged her close. "You've been through a lot. Sit down. Mom, can you grab her some water?" he asked as he looked over at Mae-Ellen.

"Coming right up," Mae-Ellen said and disappeared into the restaurant. Vicky sank down into one of the plush couches in the lobby of the inn. She sighed as Mitchell sat down beside her and wrapped his arms around her. She felt much better once she was nestled against his chest.

"And Vicky, you don't need to worry about us," Mae-Ellen said as she returned with an ice cold glass of water. "That's what I've been trying to tell you this whole time. You don't need to impress us. Honey, if you've got running water and a roof that doesn't leak then I think you're doing just fine. Besides, all that really matters is how my son feels about you. It seems pretty clear to me that he's in love."

"I am," Mitchell said with warmth and kissed Vicky firmly. When he pulled away he looked sternly into her eyes. "But if you ever send me away somewhere with Sheriff McDonnell and Rex again I will never forgive you."

"Where is Rex?" Ida asked with a smile. "I've got a story to tell him."

"He's waiting for you at your room," Mitchell said. "He wanted to surprise you."

"Maybe I'll surprise him instead," Ida grinned and hurried up the steps.

Vicky couldn't help but laugh at the shock in Mitchell's eyes. She hugged him tightly. "I'm just glad you're home," she murmured.

"Me too," he agreed. "Everyone's out looking

for Stan. We'll get him locked up soon enough."

"Uh, excuse me, Vicky?" Chef Henry asked. He had been waiting patiently for his turn to speak.

"Yes?" Vicky asked and looked over at him.

"The cake is ready," Henry smiled. "Would you like to see it?"

"Is that bad luck or something?" Maisy asked.

"Only if you knock it over," Henry laughed. "Come see, I need the bride's approval."

Vicky was relieved to escape the tension of the moment. She stepped into the kitchen and was immediately blown away by the sight of the cake. It had an intricate looped design that encircled each of the three layers. Each layer was decorated with an assortment of icing flowers that looked so real, Vicky wondered if she would ever be able to look at a plant again without thinking of cake. The gasps of approval from Mae-Ellen and Maisy let her know that they liked the cake, too.

"Oh Vicky, it's perfect," Sarah said longingly

as she looked at the cake. "Do you remember my cake?" she asked.

"I thought we were never supposed to speak of that?" Vicky asked with a laugh.

"We really shouldn't," Sarah cringed at the thought and shook her head. "Shame that Henry wasn't around then."

"I was inspired by this beautiful place that you two lovely ladies run together," Henry said kindly.

"And me, don't forget, me," Ida spoke up as she entered the kitchen. "Henry, that cake looks like it could be on the cover of a magazine. The question is, does it taste like it?" she snagged a finger full of frosting from the edge of one of the cakes.

"Aunt Ida!" Sarah and Vicky shouted at the same time.

"Woman! Out of my kitchen!" Henry shrieked and picked up a rolling pin.

"What?" Ida asked innocently and smacked her lips. "It tastes delicious."

"Run, Aunt Ida," Vicky said with a grimace as Henry rounded the butcher's block with the rolling pin in his hand.

"Eek!" Ida bolted out through the side door and across the gardens, with Henry chasing after her.

Vicky and Sarah could barely breathe between squeals of laughter. Mae-Ellen and Maisy looked horrified.

"Don't you think someone should help her?" Mae-Ellen stammered out.

"It's okay," Vicky managed to assure them between giggles. "Henry wouldn't do anything to hurt her."

"Well, at least it's not a frying pan," Mae-Ellen giggled.

"Oh yes, Vicky," Maisy said with a glimmer of mischief in her eyes. "If you ever want to see Mitchell terrified, pick up a frying pan."

"Do tell!" Vicky said hopefully.

"No you don't!" Mitchell warned and glared at his sister. "I know all about the baby pictures, too, and let me just remind you, Maisy, that for every embarrassing story you have about me, I have ten about you," he raised an eyebrow.

"Sorry," Maisy said quickly and blushed.

"I'd love to hear those, too," Vicky laughed.

"Stick around long enough and you will," Mitchell grinned. "Why don't you and Mom go meet Dad and Connor for dinner," Mitchell suggested. "I think Vicky needs the evening off."

"Off?" Vicky asked with wide eyes. "Are you kidding? I have a wedding to plan!"

Before Mitchell could answer, John, Connor, and Phil walked into the kitchen.

"Hi everyone," Phil said and then looked directly at Sarah. "You're a beautiful sight," he breathed out and walked over to her. As he wrapped his arms around her. Sarah kissed his cheek.

"You have been missed, my love," she said

with a sigh. "Rory and Ethan are quite eager to spend time with their Daddy."

"Translation, Mom needs a nap," he grinned and kissed her softly.

Mitchell raised an eyebrow, still looking steadily at Vicky, who was standing hesitantly a few feet away from him. "So, are you ready to tell me everything that happened?" he asked. Before Vicky could speak, his cell phone chimed indicating he had a text message.

"Give me a minute, guys," he said to his brother and father. "Mom and Maisy are waiting in the restaurant for you."

"Sure," John said and led Connor towards the restaurant.

"We should get the boys from Aunt Ida," Sarah said. Mitchell stared down at his phone.

Phil glanced between Vicky and Sarah, and then nodded. "All right, we better save them from whatever glitter and feathers she's coating them in."

"Vicky," Mitchell said as the kitchen emptied out. "Were you really trapped in the trunk of Stan's car?" he asked, his eyes wide.

"Not for very long," Vicky grimaced. "And we were able to get out safely."

"We?" he asked.

"Aunt Ida was there with me," she explained. "She was trying to help me solve the murder before the wedding."

"About the murder," Mitchell said and shook his head. "Can you explain to me how it ended up being Stan? I can't wrap my head around it."

"It's a very long story," Vicky said and grabbed his hand gently. "I know you must be tired..."

"Not too tired for this," he argued in return and held her hand firmly in his own. "So, what happened?"

"Arthur owed money to a loan shark, but the loan shark isn't the one who killed him. His wife Poppy wanted to sell the property she inherited, but he didn't because he knew the loan shark would want the money from it."

"So, then his wife killed him?" Mitchell asked with surprise.

"That's what I thought," Vicky said with a shake of her head. "But no, Poppy didn't do it either. She had been working with a property developer to sell the property. When the property developer found out that Arthur was refusing to sell, he decided to get rid of the problem. So, he killed Arthur and tried to frame Miriam's son for it."

"The woman who owns the party store?" Mitchell asked with disbelief. "Isn't that where you rented the wedding tent?"

"Yes," Vicky groaned. "That's how I found Arthur's body, it was wrapped up in the tent."

"No," Mitchell groaned and shook his head. "I guess we'll need a new one."

"No, it's fine," Vicky said. "Everything's fine, as long as you're here."

Mitchell smiled a little at her words. Then the smile faded. "But, why would he want to frame Miriam's son for the murder?" Mitchell asked.

"It was part of some grand plan. From what I managed to piece together I think he wanted both the Smith and Darcy properties because they are next to each other," Vicky explained. "If the party hire shop gets a bad name then they would lose business and would have to sell the shop, and it looks like they are selling the house as well. Maybe he knew, or hoped, that if they had to sell the shop they would sell their property and move elsewhere."

"Wow, a lot of trouble just for some land?" Mitchell said thoughtfully. "I'm sorry you couldn't contact me."

"At least Bobby finally managed to," Vicky smiled faintly. "And you're home now."

"Obviously, you did a great job of solving the murder," he said and slipped his arms around her waist. "And you are safe now," he added and kissed her gently.

"It's over now," Vicky murmured. "We can focus on the wedding. Right?"

"It's not quite over, is it?" he asked. "We still have to find the man who did this so we can put him behind bars."

"I know," Vicky sighed. "They haven't been able to track him down yet. Maybe he'll wait until after the wedding to resurface," she suggested hopefully.

"Maybe," he replied and rested his forehead against hers. "But no matter what we're getting married. Nothing will stop that from happening, I promise you."

Vicky smiled at his words and settled comfortably into his arms. She hoped that would prove to be true.

"All right, we have a lot of work to do," Sarah said as she walked into the room. "Enough with the mushy stuff, Vicky, save it for tomorrow. Phil has the kids, and Aunt Ida is on her way to the gardens. We're going to make sure everything is in place for tomorrow."

***

Vicky, Sarah, and Aunt Ida worked together to finish the last details of the wedding set-up that hadn't been completed. As Vicky was putting the last touches on the runner for the wedding, she heard some footsteps behind her. Her body tensed as she wondered if it could be Stan. Had he come back to finish the job? She was alone. Ida and Sarah had already gone inside to put away the materials they had used for decorating. She didn't even have her phone on her. Her heart was pounding. She cleared her throat and turned slowly to face the person standing behind her. Sheriff McDonnell stared back at her with a frown.

"Vicky," Sheriff McDonnell said as he narrowed his eyes. "I have a question for you."

"Oh," Vicky said as she looked at him. She knew he must be angry that she had tried to solve the murder. "What is it?"

"Would you like to attend the police academy?" he asked and managed to keep a straight face when he did.

Vicky smiled warmly at him as she realized he was teasing her. "No, thank you, Sir, I think I'm more suited to event planning."

"Then would you mind terribly not to parade around town as if you're a police officer?" he asked through gritted teeth. Vicky's smile faded as she realized he wasn't as amused as she had hoped he would be.

"Sure, it won't happen again," Vicky promised him, widening her deep green eyes. She hoped that it made her look innocent rather than crazy.

He stared at her for a long, heart-stopping moment. She knew that he could take Mitchell's badge if he really wanted to. "Somehow, I just don't think that I should believe you," he said and shifted his hand on his hip. "I can't say that you didn't do a good job, but you put yourself at risk because of your behavior."

"I'm sorry," Vicky said quietly.

"On the upside, my two newest officers have had some great experience, and our deputy sheriff will get the justice that he deserves. So, I guess it's all okay in the end," he said.

"I'm glad it all ended well."

"Me, too," he said as he looked into her eyes. "Just do me a favor. Next time stay out of our investigations and let us do our jobs."

"Hopefully, there won't be a next time," Vicky said with a smile.

"This is Highland," Sheriff McDonnell said with a shake of his head. "There will always be a next time. Now, make sure you get some rest tonight. Can't have you falling asleep as you walk down the aisle."

"I will," she grinned.

By the time Vicky collapsed in her bed, she was absolutely exhausted. But she still was incredibly excited for the next morning. She didn't know what might happen during the ceremony, or if she might have forgotten an important detail or two, but she did know one thing for sure. She was going to marry the love of her life. Despite investigating a murder and putting herself in danger he still loved her. He wanted her, as she was, and had no desire to change her. That meant a lot to Vicky. As she drifted off to sleep her mind was filled with thoughts of doves, and exploding cakes. She might have even witnessed a firework or two.

Chapter Eleven

The next morning was a bustle of activity. Vicky shared a delicious breakfast with Mae-Ellen, Maisy, Sarah, and Ida. Then the four of them began preparing Vicky for the wedding. Despite all of the planning, Vicky felt overwhelmed. It was a very special day, but not because of the flowers, or the ceremony. It was special because it was the day that she was going to promise to spend the rest of her life with Mitchell, a man she couldn't imagine ever living without.

By the time her make-up was done, and her brown hair was swirled up and pinned to the top of her head, she was shivering with nervousness and excitement. Maisy and Mae-Ellen left to check on Mitchell, and Sarah ducked out to check on Rory and Ethan who were serving as flower-boy and ring-bearer. Alone with her aunt, Vicky tried to take a deep breath. She stood in front of the floor to ceiling mirror on her bedroom door.

"What do you think, Aunt Ida?" Vicky asked as she smoothed down the skirt of her ivory gown.

"I think it needs more color," Aunt Ida said with disdain.

"Oh no," Vicky laughed as she turned to face her aunt.

"Your bouquet," Ida said and handed her the bundle of flowers that matched each layer on the cake. Vicky clasped it tightly and looked into Ida's eyes. She could feel tears forming.

"Vicky, what's wrong?" Ida asked and touched her cheek lightly. "Are those happy tears or sad tears?"

"A little of both, maybe," Vicky said in a whisper. "I'm so happy to be marrying Mitchell, but..."

"You wish your parents were here," Ida supplied and hugged her gently. "I know, sweetie, I wish they were, too."

"I didn't think it would be so hard to walk down the aisle alone," Vicky murmured.

"Alone?" Ida smiled as she pulled away from her and looked into her eyes. "I was kind of hoping that you might not want to be alone."

"What do you mean?" Vicky asked as she delicately dabbed at her eyes.

"To be honest, Vicky," Ida said. "I don't have any children of my own, and Sarah is already married. I was hoping..."

"Would you really?" Vicky asked, her eyes widening. "You would walk me down the aisle?"

"I would be honored," Ida replied with warmth in her voice. "If that's what you want, of course."

"Yes, it is, I couldn't think of a more perfect person to walk down the aisle with me," Vicky said happily. "Thank you, Aunt Ida!"

"Only happy tears, okay?" she asked with a smile.

"Only happy tears," Vicky agreed.

"I'll check on the musicians," Ida said as she walked towards the door. "I'm sure Sarah will want to help you with your train and veil."

"Thank you again, Aunt Ida," Vicky said as she watched her aunt step out of the room. She was thrilled that she would be escorting her down the aisle. As Ida stepped out of the room, Sarah stepped in.

"Hey there, beautiful blushing bride," Sarah smiled as she closed the door behind her.

"How is it out there?" Vicky asked nervously.

"Everything is perfect," Sarah assured her.

"The musicians are playing for the guests and everyone is beginning to take their seats," Sarah smiled. "This is it, Vicky. This is really it. Are you ready?"

"I think so," Vicky replied and clutched her bouquet tighter.

"Don't worry, no one ever really is," Sarah

said and hugged her gently. But I couldn't think of a more perfect person for you to spend the rest of your life with."

"Me neither," Vicky agreed. "So, why does it feel like I'm going to explode and pass out at the same time?" she cringed.

"Oh honey, that's how it's supposed to feel," Sarah promised her with a laugh. "Listen, Phil and I were talking, and he mentioned that if you would like, he'd be happy to walk you down the aisle. I know it wouldn't be the same but..."

"Oh wow," Vicky said with a wide smile. "That is so kind of him to offer."

"You know Phil loves you," Sarah said and squeezed her hands. "I know that he would be honored."

"Thank you," Vicky said warmly. "But Aunt Ida already offered."

"That explains the tuxedo dress," Sarah burst out laughing.

"Wait, what?" Vicky asked with wide eyes.

"You'll see," Sarah grinned. "Oh Vicky, it's so wonderful to see you so happy. It's time, you better get out there," Sarah hugged her again. Sarah delicately drew the veil down over Vicky's face. She straightened it until it was resting just right. Vicky stood up and Sarah clipped the train to the back of the dress.

"Do you remember when you did this for me?" Sarah asked.

"Yes," Vicky giggled. "I stuck you in the backside with the pin."

"Oh yes! I had almost forgotten about that!" Sarah laughed. "Well, I guess it's time to return the favor."

"No!" Vicky laughed and jumped away.

"I'm just kidding," Sarah promised her and opened the door for Vicky. When Vicky stepped out through the door, Ida was waiting for her on the other side. She had changed out of her flashy purple dress, and was now wearing a finely tailored tuxedo dress, just as Sarah had said she was. It looked exquisite on Ida, and Vicky couldn't help but shake her head at how beautiful her aunt looked. Ida straightened her bow tie and then extended her hand to Vicky.

"Time to get this party started," Ida said and wiggled her bottom back and forth.

"Nice, Aunt Ida," Sarah said with a laugh.

Ida and Vicky walked to the side door of the lobby. Outside, Vicky could see that all of her guests had taken their seats. The garden was filled with smiling faces, bright blossoming flowers, and flowing live music. But Vicky barely noticed any of that. All she saw was Mitchell, in his suit, standing nervously at the end of the aisle. He kept shifting from one foot to the other, as if he didn't trust the ground not to disappear. The minister was talking quietly with him.

Vicky assumed he was attempting to calm Mitchell down. Vicky continued to watch him for a long moment. Her heart skipped a beat as she knew this was the last time she would be looking at him as her fiancé. From now on he would be her husband, a man she could trust, and who she knew would stand by her no matter what happened in their lives.

Rory and Ethan were already making their way down the aisle in their little tuxedos. Vicky had never seen anything more adorable. For every flower that Rory tossed on the ground, Ethan was walking behind him trying to pick them up.

"Rory, stop making such a mess, this is Aunt Vicky's wedding," Ethan fussed. Vicky had to hide a grin.

Ida gave her hand a soft squeeze. Vicky smiled at her. Then they both began walking towards the aisle. As soon as the musicians noticed their approach they began playing the Wedding March. Vicky's heart began to race, as she knew this was finally it, there was no turning back, unless of course she decided to run. She could go back to her single life, with no commitments. She could be free to roam and rest as she pleased. She could move to any place in the world, without having to consult another person about the decision. But as Mitchell turned to watch her walk down the aisle, all Vicky could think of was the one place she wanted to be, in his arms. The wide smile that Mitchell offered her led her to believe that he was thinking something very similar. As she reached the end of the aisle, he automatically reached for her hands. Ida gave Vicky a quick hug and a peck on the cheek before turning her over to Mitchell. Mitchell's eyes were filled with love as he held her hands gently in his own.

"You look amazing," he whispered before the minister could begin speaking.

Vicky lost herself in Mitchell's loving gaze. She was so enraptured by it that she barely heard the words of the minister as he rambled through the ceremony. Vicky didn't need to hear any special words, or make any special vows to know that Mitchell would be with her for life. She could see his promise in the way that he looked at her, and it made her feel like the luckiest woman on the face of the earth.

What Vicky didn't notice was a man walking towards the ceremony. She didn't notice that he was holding a gun at his side. She didn't notice that he was the murderer who had her locked in the trunk of his car less than twenty-four hours before. She didn't see that he was raising his gun with the intention of shooting her in the middle of the ceremony. Luckily, there was one person who did see him. One person who was always looking out for Vicky, no matter what was happening around her.

"Not so fast," Ida growled and stuck her foot out into the aisle before Stan could make his way down it. She grabbed the hand holding the gun and pointed it down as Stan fell face first into the grass. She lithely jumped on top of him and pinned his arms behind his back. When the other guests at the wedding began to notice what was happening, Ida put her finger to her lips and tilted her head towards the bride and groom. The guests did their best to contain their surprise. The minister stuttered over a few words as Aunt Ida escorted Stan to Sheriff McDonnell who tugged him towards the parking lot. Despite all that had occurred, Vicky and Mitchell were still gazing steadily into each other's eyes.

The minister looked warily beyond them, towards Ida. Ida nodded towards him. He smiled and continued the ceremony.

"I now pronounce you, husband and wife," he said warmly.

Vicky looked up at him startled. Mitchell blinked.

"Already?" he asked, drawing a smattering of laughter from the guests.

"Don't worry this is the best part," Vicky grinned and leaned close to him. Mitchell met her with a soft and savoring kiss.

Everyone in attendance cheered and clapped for the new couple. Rory and Ethan hollered and jumped up and down. Sarah was too busy crying to make a sound. Phil hugged her close.

As Vicky turned around she saw Rex take

Aunt Ida into his arms and hold her tight. She saw Mitchell's mother smiling proudly at them both. For the first time in a very long time, Vicky felt complete, and as if she had everything in the world to celebrate. As long as the wedding cake didn't explode.

The End

More Cozy Mysteries by Cindy Bell

Dune House Cozy Mystery Series

Seaside Secrets

Boats and Bad Guys

Treasured History

Hidden Hideaways

Dodgy Dealings

Heavenly Highland Inn Cozy Mystery Series

Murdering the Roses

Dead in the Daisies

Killing the Carnations

Drowning the Daffodils

Suffocating the Sunflowers

Books, Bullets and Blooms

A Deadly serious Gardening Contest

Wendy the Wedding Planner Cozy Mystery Series

Matrimony, Money and Murder

Chefs, Ceremonies and Crimes

Knives and Nuptials

Bekki the Beautician Cozy Mystery Series

Hairspray and Homicide

A Dyed Blonde and a Dead Body

Mascara and Murder

Pageant and Poison

Conditioner and a Corpse

Mistletoe, Makeup and Murder

Hairpin, Hair Dryer and Homicide

Blush, a Bride and a Body

Shampoo and a Stiff

Cosmetics, a Cruise and a Killer

Lipstick, a Long Iron and Lifeless

Camping, Concealer and Criminals

Printed in Great Britain
by Amazon